"There's nothing y[...]

"I wouldn't dream of it." [...]
of keeping Dani from joi[...]
he was almost looking forward to another meeting
with the fiery lawyer. Ever since his wife's death, his
friends and family had treated him with kid gloves—
always careful with how they spoke, what they said.

Dani, on the other hand, had gotten in his face,
telling him what she thought without holding back.
That kind of forthrightness was refreshing and, he
was shocked to realize, a bit of a turn-on.

Of course, it wasn't going to lead to anything; he
was already overwhelmed with running a business
and caring for his daughters, not to mention the
new responsibility of being a mentor to a troubled
boy. The very last thing he needed was one more
complication in his life—romantic or otherwise.

Still, there was no harm in looking. No harm at all.

PROPOSALS IN PARADISE:
True love on bended knee!

Dear Reader,

I hope you are as excited as I am to return to Paradise Isle! Some familiar faces are waiting to greet you, including Dani Post, who first appeared in *Do You Take This Daddy?* and then returned in *A Wedding Worth Waiting For*. This time we find out that she has a secret she's been hiding from us, and from her friends and family. Like most secrets, keeping this one hasn't been easy. Battling PTSD while trying to keep up appearances is taking its toll. Thankfully, she has Tyler Jackson on her side!

Tyler is a widower with young twins who sees what others don't—that Dani is dealing with something traumatic and needs support. But just because he cares for her doesn't mean they don't butt heads on occasion! Neither one is afraid to speak their mind, maybe because after living through trauma—be that an assault or a loss of a loved one—you learn that life is too short to do anything less than speak the truth. But despite their differences (or maybe because of them?) they find they are the perfect team.

As you read I hope you'll let me know if any of Dani or Tyler's struggles resonate with you— I love hearing from my readers! Find me on Facebook at Facebook.com/katiemeyerbooks, or you can follow me on Instagram as katiemeyerbooks and Twitter as @ktgrok. To get information on new releases and contests, sign up for my mailing list at katiemeyerbooks.com.

Happy reading!

Katie Meyer

The Groom's Little Girls

—

Katie Meyer

⟨H⟩**HARLEQUIN**®SPECIAL EDITION®

Recycling programs
for this product may
not exist in your area.

ISBN-13: 978-0-373-62342-6

The Groom's Little Girls

Copyright © 2017 by Katie Meyer

Printed in U.S.A.

Katie Meyer is a Florida native with a firm belief in happy endings. A former veterinary technician and dog trainer, she now spends her days homeschooling her children, writing and snuggling with her pets. Her guilty pleasures include good chocolate, *Downton Abbey* and cheap champagne. Preferably all at once. She looks to her parents' whirlwind romance and her own happy marriage for her romantic inspiration.

Books by Katie Meyer

Harlequin Special Edition

Proposals in Paradise
A Wedding Worth Waiting For

Paradise Animal Clinic
Do You Take This Daddy?
A Valentine for the Veterinarian
The Puppy Proposal

This book is dedicated to all those who have been mistreated because of their gender or sexual identity, and to anyone struggling with mental health issues, especially PTSD.

Chapter One

Why were the good-looking ones always jerks?

That was the thought circling through lawyer Dani Post's mind as Tyler Jackson made his way to the witness box. Yes, he was gorgeous, with ice-blue eyes, short, cropped blond hair and an athletic build that had the middle-aged courtroom reporter nearly drooling as she typed. But he obviously lacked a shred of human decency, as far as Dani could tell, and she'd had more than enough experience with men like that. It was because of him that the little boy at her side was trembling with fear, his sweaty hand clenched around her own.

Kevin McCarthy, a precocious nine-year-old, had been caught stealing a baseball bat from the toy store that Tyler owned. Obviously he shouldn't have done it, but there were extenuating circumstances, not the least of which was that Kevin was a foster kid who'd been through more trauma in his short life than most adults could even imagine. The boy had just wanted to be able to join in the pick-up baseball games at the park, and knowing his foster parents couldn't afford a new bat he'd grabbed one out of desperation, hoping that it would help him fit in with his peers. Dani didn't condone his actions, but surely the coldhearted toy-store owner could have handled it without going to the cops! He could have just made the boy return the bat or spoken to his foster parents. Maybe had him do some chores around the shop. But instead he'd pressed charges against a kid barely big enough to see over the witness box.

And now Kevin was her very first guardian *ad litem* case. Guardians *ad litem*, GALs for short, were adult volunteers who were assigned to children involved in the family court system, to advocate for their rights and help make what could be a frightening process easier for the child. Originally they had only been assigned in abuse cases, but Palmetto County, Florida, had recently expanded the program to all foster children, to help them navigate the family court system. Dani's job was to help him understand what was happening, and to speak out on the child's behalf as his representative. And now, with Kevin facing criminal charges, she was also acting as his guide through the juvenile justice system.

A legal background like Dani's, although not necessary, was helpful, and the program director had assured Dani that even though she'd only been practicing a few years she was more than qualified. But nothing in the training program had prepared her for how emotional it would be, and how hard. The very thing that had drawn her to the program, her understanding of what it felt like to be vulnerable and powerless, was what made doing the job so heartbreaking. When she looked at Kevin she didn't see a case or a volunteer project. She saw a frightened little boy who had made a mistake he was very sorry for. He was just a kid who needed a break—someone to stand by him and believe in him. Sitting next to her, legs dangling several inches above the ground, he seemed so small and vulnerable. And she knew too well what it was like to feel vulnerable.

Unfortunately, the outcome was out of her hands. Her role in this case was as an advisor and sounding board. She could explain things to Kevin, but she had no say in what happened. If this had been a custody hearing, she would have presented her opinion to the judge, but in a criminal case she was on the sidelines, there for moral support as much as anything. So she bit her tongue, held Kevin's hand and glared daggers at Tyler Jackson.

A few minutes later, he finished speaking and, at the judge's direction, left the witness box and headed for the back of the courtroom. Dani found her eyes drawn to him as he strode down the center of the room, passing within inches of the table where she sat. As if feeling the intensity of her gaze, he glanced down at her briefly. Then he was past her, and a minute later she heard the heavy doors of the courtroom thud close.

"Good riddance," she mumbled under her breath. Something about him made her nervous, almost restless. She'd like to blame it on her anger at him for pressing charges, but she'd noticed it the moment she saw him in the courtroom, well before she'd realized who he was. No, it was something intrinsic to him, and not the situation, that made her skin tingle in awareness. The same hyperawareness she felt before a big electrical storm, telling her lightning was about to strike.

It was probably just that he seemed too handsome, too sure of himself, too confident, which were all characteristics that had led her astray in the past. Or maybe she'd met him before, and it was some weird recognition kicking in, although she hadn't been in the toy store he ran that she could remember. She tended to shop online, late at night when insomnia struck.

But whatever the reason, he was gone now and she could turn all her attention back to Kevin and the trial. The judge, a matronly looking woman in her mid-fifties or so, finished writing something on the papers in front of her, then cleared her throat before turning toward the defense table. Kevin was instructed to stand, and he did, his freckles stark against his suddenly pale skin.

Dani felt her own pulse racing, and forced herself to smile, trying to send positive thoughts even as she waited for the judge's decision. Luckily, the Honorable Sheila Graves lived up to her reputation as both efficient and compassionate, delivering her verdict without further delay—probation, and participation in the county mentoring program for at-risk youth.

Dani let out a shaky breath and turned to Kevin, who looked a bit shell-shocked at the decision. "Do you understand what she said?"

He started to nod, then shook his head in confusion. "I don't have to go to jail?"

She swallowed past the lump in her throat. "No, big guy, you don't have to go to jail. You got probation— that just means you have to be on your best behavior, and not break any more laws. You can do that, no problem, right?"

He nodded, more confidently this time. "And I have to have a mentor."

She smiled. "That's right. Do you know what a mentor is?"

"Not really."

"It's just a person, someone older and maybe a bit wiser, who will be your friend. Someone to hang out with you, give you advice, someone you can talk to about things that are bugging you."

Some of the stiffness went out of his stance. "That sounds okay, I guess. But can I still hang out with you, too?"

Dani felt her heart squeeze. He tried to pretend he was tough, but deep down he was still just a scared little boy. Putting an arm over his shoulders, she guided him toward the back doors, where his foster parents were waiting. "Of course. You didn't think you could get rid of me that easily, did you?"

"So you'll come with me to meet the mentor person?"

She hesitated. It really wasn't her place, and the mentor might want one-on-one time to build a rapport.

"Please?"

Tears welled up in big brown eyes, and she knew she couldn't say no. Whoever the mentor was, surely they'd understand. And if not, they'd just have to deal with it. "Of course I'll go with you. Wouldn't miss it for the world."

* * *

Dani spent the remainder of the afternoon holed up in her office, trying to concentrate on the probate paperwork she'd promised to finish by tomorrow. But no matter how hard she tried, she couldn't keep her mind on her work. Estate planning, although important, didn't compare to the challenge of trial law, and on days like today she missed her old job. More than that, she missed who she'd been, before she'd lost faith in the system and herself.

Restless, she found her eyes drawn to the window yet again. It was a gorgeous spring day, and as usual there was a crowd of kids at the ice-cream parlor across the street, eagerly lapping up their after-school treats while their moms congregated in the shade of an awning. Usually she found the view soothing, a reminder of all the goodness in life, but today it was like a punch in the gut. Kevin should be doing stuff like that— eating ice cream and laughing with friends. Not spending the day in court. And as much as his foster parents, the Cunninghams, wanted to do right by him, she couldn't picture the elderly couple taking him for ice cream after school or pitching baseballs to him in the park. Maybe his new mentor would help with that kind of thing. But even that was a temporary fix to a much larger problem. One she had no idea how to solve.

And staring at the same paragraph of legalese for the fifteenth time wasn't going to change anything. She shoved the papers into her briefcase and decided to finish up at home. Maybe a brisk walk would clear her head and help her focus. A run would be even better, but her work clothes weren't exactly conducive to that, so a walk would have to do. Snagging her purse, she ducked into the room next door, where her father was seated at an oversized desk covered in yellow legal pads. "I'm going to head out, and work on this at home."

Her father's eyebrows arched. She never left early. "Everything okay?"

"Sure, just a bit of spring fever."

Worry lines creased his forehead. They'd always had a close bond, but in the year since she'd returned home it had become a bit strained. Not because of their working relationships—the letterhead might carry the name of Phillip Post, but he treated Dani as if she were a full partner. No, it was more likely because he sensed there were things she hadn't told him about her time in Jacksonville and her reasons for coming home. Finally, he sighed and nodded. "If you need anything, call. I'm happy to help."

Impulsively, she rounded the desk and gave him a hug. "I know you are. I'm lucky to have you."

He smiled at the sudden show of affection. "Yes, you are. And don't you forget it!" His eyes twinkled. "Now go, and let an old man concentrate on his work."

She smiled, feeling a bit lighter, and made her way out of the small but well-appointed office, waving to her mom, who worked part-time as the receptionist and was on the phone discussing appointment times with someone. She really was lucky to have such a close family. Some of her friends thought it was a bit odd that she didn't mind spending her days with not one but both of her parents, but they got along well and so far it hadn't been a problem. She liked them, and although her sister, Mollie, had butted heads with them on a regular basis, Dani had been fortunate enough to always have a good relationship with them. Working in the guardian *ad litem* program, seeing how many people didn't get to grow up with a loving family, had led her to a new appreciation of her own circumstances.

Kevin might look up to her, but she found she was equally inspired by him and his ability to hold on to hope despite his circumstances. He'd lost his mother a year ago to an opioid overdose, after she'd been prescribed the medication for a back injury. He'd never known his father, and when he ended up in the foster-care system it was discovered the man that had sired him was in prison, serving out a twenty-year sentence. Once in the system Kevin had bounced around from one temporary placement to another before ending up with the Cunninghams. Senior citizens, they had been fostering kids for nearly a decade, ever since their son had moved to California for a job in the tech industry. They'd missed having family, and foster care had given them an outlet for the love they were eager to share.

In many ways, it was the perfect placement for a grieving boy like Kevin, but as wonderful as the Cunninghams were, they were getting on in age, and Dani suspected that keeping up with an active little boy was taking its toll. What he really needed was his parents, but they were gone and the chances of a boy his age being adopted were slim from what the caseworker had told her. The whole thing just sucked. But dwelling on it wasn't doing Kevin or her mood any good. She needed to snap out of her funk if she was going to do right by her clients and get any work done today at all.

On a whim, she crossed the street and turned left instead of right. The big trail that wound through the park would take her only a little out of her way, and the extra sunshine and fresh air would be worth the lost time. Turning east off of Lighthouse Avenue, Paradise Isle's version of Main Street, she walked the two blocks to Pelican Park and felt her spirits lift. Dozens of children were playing a chaotic game of dodgeball on the big green field near the entrance. Peals of laughter alternated with shrieks of indignation as the kids scrambled in the thick grass. On the other side of the trail squirrels played their own games, fighting over acorns and chasing each other through the tree boughs.

Continuing down the paved path, she passed the basketball court, empty now but sure to be bustling once the high school let out, and then the baseball fields. A group of kids, maybe late-elementary or early-middle-school-aged, were playing a pick-up game on the closest diamond. She squinted, shading her eyes from the sun. Were these the boys Kevin had been trying to impress? Had they teased him for not being able to afford his own bat, or had he just imagined their judgment? He hadn't wanted to give details and she hadn't pushed. In the end, it didn't really matter.

Pushing on, the playground finally came into view. It was situated near the far entrance of the park and had been rebuilt recently. Gone was the scorching hot metal slide she remembered from her youth along with the rest of the old equipment—it had all been replaced with more colorful, and no doubt safer, modern play equipment. Domes of red and blue shaded the ladders and slides, offering protection from the tropical sun. Benches full of watchful parents circled the perimeter, giving wearied moms and dads a chance to socialize a bit while keeping an eye on rambunctious little ones. That part of the scene, at least, was similar to what she remembered. Her mom had often sat on those same benches after walking to the park with Dani and Mollie. On the weekends her father had come, too, often taking the whole family for ice cream afterward.

Smiling at the memory, she was almost to the park gates when the sound of crying stopped her. Glancing back, she saw a little girl with blond pigtails, no more than five years old, sobbing hysterically at the foot of the swing set. Standing over her was a man, one with an oddly familiar build, his back toward her. Without thought, her feet started moving in their direction, the little girl's cries spurring her on. Rounding a bench, she was about to offer assistance when she realized why the man looked familiar. It was the toy-store owner from the trial! What was he doing here—harassing random preschoolers?

"Haven't you upset enough children today?" He looked up, and again she was hit by that feeling of unease that she'd felt in the courtroom, like her skin was suddenly a size too tight. Ignoring the feeling, and him, she looked down to the girl, who had stopped crying at Dani's interruption. "Are you okay, honey? Is he bothering you?"

"I'm okay. Daddy was just kissing my boo-boo." She pointed to a slightly skinned knee. "My sister, Amy, is the one that was bothering me." She glared back toward the swings, where an equally adorable and nearly identical girl glared back at her. "She pushed my swing too hard and I felled off."

Dani did a double take, looking from one angelic face to the other, then slowly turned back to the man in the middle of it all. "Your daddy?"

Tyler Jackson, the coldhearted man who had pressed

charges against a nine-year-old boy and then testified against him in court, was a father?

Tyler helped Adelaide, the younger and more dramatic of his twins, up off the ground. "It's barely a scratch, you'll be fine. Now go play—we've got to head back soon. And Amy," he said, shifting his attention to the other girl, who was trying and failing to look innocent of all wrongdoing, "be nice to your sister. I'll be watching."

"Okaaay!" she huffed, clearly offended at his implication that she needed watching. Full of sass, that one was. Between her newfound bossiness and her sister's histrionics, he was starting to feel like he'd never get the hang of this single-parenting thing. Just as soon as he thought he had them figured out, they grew and changed and confused him all over again. Where were the sweet little girls that had cooed at him from their cribs? Of course, those days hadn't been easy, either; raising infant twins never was. But at least he'd had help then. Jennifer, his late wife, had done the bulk of the caregiving, leaving him to enjoy the fun parts of fatherhood.

But Jennifer had been gone for two years now, taken by ovarian cancer faster than he could have imagined. And he was going to have to fill her shoes along with his own, no matter how hard it was. Often the weight of the responsibility felt like it might crush him, but the girls were still the two best things in his life, and he was a smart enough man to know that he was luckier than most.

"You have kids?"

He turned back to face the woman that had approached Adelaide when she'd been crying. She looked familiar, and it hit him. She had been in the courtroom today, sitting with the boy he'd caught shoplifting. Maybe she was a relative? He extended a hand, falling back on the manners his grandmother had ingrained in him. "I do. Name's Tyler Jackson, and those little munchkins are Amy and Adelaide. I'm sorry if they upset you. They normally get along pretty well but you know how siblings can be."

She ignored his hand and stared up at him. She was probably a good six inches shorter than him, and less than half his weight, but if she noticed the size difference she didn't let on. Instead, she stabbed a finger into his chest and lit into him like an angry mother hen. "I know exactly who you are, Mr. Jackson. You're the man that tried to get a confused little boy, an orphan no less, put behind bars over a measly baseball bat. That's who you are!"

He kept his tone even, not rising to the bait. "I suppose that's one way to look at it. And you are?"

"Dani Post, Kevin's guardian *ad litem*." She looked fierce, he'd give her that, with her dark hair blowing in the breeze like a mane and her dark eyes snapping in anger. But at least she'd stopped poking him.

"Well, Ms. Post, I'm very sorry about the boy's family situation, but that doesn't excuse stealing."

She glared. "Of course not. But he needs help, not legal trouble."

He crossed his arms and settled onto his heels. "And I happen to think the legal system is the best way to make sure he gets that help. He's going into the mentor program, right?"

She nodded, but didn't look any less upset. "You

couldn't have known that would be the final result, though."

"Actually, the prosecutor's office assured me that was the most likely scenario. And I've had some experience with juvenile courts—they don't go throwing young kids in jail if they don't have to."

"Thank goodness for that." She tossed a strand of hair out of her eyes. "But he's had a hard time, and deserves a second chance."

"And he'll get it."

"No thanks to you."

Tyler checked to be sure his daughters were still safely playing on the swings, then turned back to the angry woman in front of him. Dressed smartly in black slacks and a crimson blouse, she looked like she should be in a boardroom, not at a playground. But if she was a lawyer, that made sense. As did her confrontational communication style. But he wasn't a witness on the stand, and she didn't intimidate him. Impressed, and even a bit attracted, but not intimidated. "Actually, I intend to be a very large part of it. I'm going to be his mentor."

"You're what?" He could almost taste the anger and frustration pouring off of her as she digested that bit of news. "Haven't you done enough damage? What more do you want?"

"To keep him from making any more mistakes. Listen, I get that you are worried about him, and that's admirable. And I'm sure it helps. But a boy that age needs someone who can teach him how to be a man."

"And what makes you the right person for the job?"

"Nothing really, except I'm willing to do it. I turned him in because I thought it was the best way to teach him a lesson, to keep him from getting into more trouble down the road. I made a few mistakes of my own at that age, and someone stepped in and helped me out. I figure now it's my turn."

She blinked at him, a wary respect replacing the look of disgust she'd worn only a few minutes ago. "Well, I hope that's the truth. But you should know, he's asked me to be there when he meets with you, and I intend to do just that. And there's nothing you can do to stop me." With that she spun on her high-heeled shoe and strode off.

"I wouldn't dream of it," he said to himself, watching her retreat. No, he had no intention of keeping her from joining them; in fact he found he was almost looking forward to another meeting with the fiery lawyer. Ever since his wife's death, his friends and family had treated him with kid gloves—always careful how they spoke, what they said. No one wanted to upset the grieving widower. He appreciated the sentiment, but a man didn't want to be handled like a child.

Dani, on the other hand, had gotten in his face, telling him what she thought without holding back. That kind of forthrightness was refreshing and, he was shocked to realize, a bit of a turn-on. He hadn't had a physical reaction to a woman in longer than he could remember. He'd had chances; plenty had been interested in stepping into his late wife's place. But none of them had sparked the kind of attraction he'd felt just now.

Of course, it wasn't going to lead to anything: he was already overwhelmed with running a business and caring for his daughters, not to mention the new responsibility of being a mentor to a troubled boy. The very last thing he needed was one more complication in his life—romantic or otherwise. But still, there was no harm in looking. No harm at all.

Chapter Two

Dani parked her red convertible, a gift to herself when she'd been hired at Whitehorn and Watts right out of law school, in the gravel lot in front of the Paradise Wildlife Rehabilitation Center. Making the payments was a bit harder on her current, significantly lower salary, but she couldn't quite bring herself to trade it in for something more economical. From the backseat Kevin peppered her with questions, anxious to see the animals, and probably equally anxious about coming face-to-face with Tyler Jackson. Dani had worried that the boy would balk at the idea of the shopkeeper being his mentor, but she'd assured Kevin that the man wasn't looking to punish him, just help him. Hopefully that was the truth. She'd been up half the night wondering if she should have petitioned the court for a different mentor, one not associated with the case. But it was too late now, and with Kevin being so brave, she didn't want to undermine his confidence by backing out.

"What about tigers? Do they have tigers?" A glance in the rearview mirror showed Kevin practically bouncing in his booster seat as he swiveled his head from side to side, trying to spy one of the animals she'd told him the center housed.

"Nope, no tigers. Remember, I told you they take care of native species, animals that live in Florida naturally. But they do have a panther, which is kind of a cousin to a tiger. His name is Simba."

"Okay, that's cool. Can I pet him?"

"Definitely not." She got out of the car and opened the back door, leaning in to look him in the eyes. "You don't touch any of the animals unless an adult says it is okay, got it?"

He nodded solemnly, his serious expression at odds with the sparkle in his eyes. Seeing him this excited, this happy, made her heart flip-flop in her chest. Rumpling his hair quickly, she backed out of the way so he could get out of the car, then led him to the main building, where Tyler was supposed to meet them.

The low-slung brown-and-green wooden building nearly blended into the woods around it. Groupings of native plants, many chosen for their attractiveness to butterflies, lined the path to the front door. Set on land designated as part of the Paradise Wildlife Refuge, the rehab center served a vital purpose. Injured animals were treated at the hospital on site, and then released when they were ready. Animals that couldn't be released were allowed to live out their lives at the center, where they were cared for by the staff and a dedicated team of volunteers including Dani and her sister. Dylan Turner, the director, had become a close friend. Seeing how gentle the big surfer dude was with injured animals had put her at ease around him during a time when her defenses had been at an all-time high.

Opening the door, she spied him sitting at his desk, behind the big reception counter that separated the public area from the staff office. "Hey, Dylan! Working hard?"

Shaking his blond hair out of his eyes, he smiled wanly. "Always. You know how busy spring is...lots of babies being brought in this time of year."

"Any we can see today?"

"Sure, I've got a possum back there to show you two, if your friend there would like to see it."

"I'm sure he would." She gestured between them and made introductions. "Kevin, this is Mr. Turner. He runs this place. Dylan, this is Kevin. We are meeting a new friend, and then we'd love a tour, right, Kevin?"

"Definitely!"

Perfect. When she'd talked to Tyler on the phone to discuss possible outings, he'd suggested the ice-cream parlor on Lighthouse Avenue. Which probably would have been fine. But this seemed so much cooler for a kid, and she'd convinced Tyler it was the better choice.

The bell over the front door rang, cutting off her mental self-congratulations. Looking more casual but just as intimidating, Tyler walked in wearing cargo shorts and a plain white T-shirt, dark glasses hiding the piercing blue eyes she remembered from the courtroom. Beside her, Kevin crowded closer. Clearly uneasy, she had a sense that only his pride was keeping him from hiding behind her.

Dylan, picking up on the sudden tension, left his

desk and came to stand between Kevin and Tyler. "Everything okay?" His words were for Dani, but his eyes darted between the obviously scared little boy and the man that seemed to be the cause of his fear.

"Everything is fine." She laid a hand on Kevin's shoulder in what she hoped was a comforting gesture, and forced a smile. "This is Tyler Jackson, and he's here to have some fun with Kevin and me, right?"

Kevin made the barest of nods, but Tyler, to her surprise, broke into a grin and crouched down at the boy's level. "That's right. As long as that's okay with Kevin. Can I come with you guys?"

The boy's eyes widened. He clearly hadn't expected to be consulted. "Um, yeah, it's okay I guess."

"Thanks, I've been looking forward to it." He straightened and offered a hand to Dylan, who smiled and returned the gesture. "Nice to meet you."

"You, too. I'm Dylan, by the way. If you want to wait a bit, I can give you a guided tour myself. Otherwise Dani knows the place pretty well, and I'm sure she can show you around."

Dylan was famous for getting caught up in his work; if they waited for him they might never get to see anything. "I think we can manage on our own, right, guys?"

"Sure," Kevin agreed, no doubt eager to get on with it. She glanced at Tyler, who nodded his assent.

"All right then, let's get started. Dylan, where would we find that baby possum you were telling us about?"

"In the main treatment room, in one of the cages on the back wall. Just don't take him out—he's little but his teeth are sharp."

"We'll start there then, thanks." She opened the half

door that led to the office, then led the way through the back door into the heart of the rehab center. Kevin trotted at her heels, with Tyler bringing up the rear.

"Wow, this is like a real doctor's office." Running over to the long stainless-steel table, he eyed the tubes and dials of an anesthesia machine. "Do they do surgery on alligators and stuff here?"

"Um, maybe?" Dani usually helped with the fundraising side of things, not the hands-on, messy stuff. "We can ask Dylan on the way out, or I can call my sister later. She'd know. She volunteers here a lot. In fact, she even trained that panther I was telling you about."

"Cool!"

"That is pretty cool," Tyler agreed, making his way toward the bank of cages Dylan had said the possum was in. "I've never seen a panther close up."

"Dani says panthers and tigers are cousins. Do you think that's true?"

"It is. All cats are related in some way, even house cats." Tyler had Kevin's full attention now. "My little girls have been begging me for a kitten. Maybe I should ask if they have a spare panther here. What do you think?"

Kevin giggled, his nostrils crinkling. "Not a good idea."

Tyler scratched his head in mock confusion. "No? Not the same thing?"

"Uh-uh. You had better get them a regular kitten."

"You're probably right. Oh, well." Dylan pointed to a cage just to the right of where they were standing. "Hey, I think I found that baby possum."

Kevin rushed over, his earlier nervousness forgotten. "Oh, wow, look how small it is! He's really funny-looking!"

Dani joined them, peering over Kevin's head at what looked like an overgrown rat with an extralong pink snout. "Whoa, he is pretty unusual. But he's just a baby. Maybe he'll get better looking when he grows up."

"How come he's all alone in there? Where's his mom? Is she in another cage?"

Dani winced. "No, it's just the baby that is here. That happens sometimes. But they're going to take good care of it, don't worry."

"But what happened to his mom?" His voice rose in pitch. "What happened to her?"

"I don't know for sure, honey, but she—she probably died. Most of the baby animals they get here are brought in because the parents aren't there to care for them anymore."

"So he's an orphan?"

Tears filled his eyes, and Dani felt her own welling up in response. What on earth had she been thinking, bringing him to see orphaned animals? "Yes, he is. But he's going to be okay. Dylan and the other workers will make sure of it. And as soon as he's big enough they'll let him go, back in the wild." Maybe knowing there was a happy ending waiting for the possum would help smooth things over.

"They're going to abandon him? On his own? That's mean. Mean, mean, mean!" Kevin stomped his foot with each word, his face scrunched up to the point his freckles were running together. "I hate this place. Take me home. Now!" And with that he ran out the nearest door.

* * *

Tyler grabbed Dani's arm as she started to chase after the boy. "Is it safe out there? All the animals are in enclosures, I mean?"

She tugged, trying to break his grip. "Yes, of course it's safe. But he's upset. I need to go to him, and explain—"

"Fine, but let him have a minute to himself first. He's upset, yes, but he's going to be even more embarrassed for crying in front of us. Give him a little time to calm down. Trust me."

She kept her eyes on the door, but stopped trying to pull away. "One minute, but then I'm going after him."

"We'll both go."

Dani ran her hands through her shoulder-length dark hair, frustration and regret clear as day on her face. "I can't believe I was such an idiot. I just thought he'd like to see cute baby animals. Everyone likes baby animals, right?"

It seemed like a rhetorical question, but he nodded anyway.

"It never occurred to me that he'd focus in on them being orphans. Of course, it should have." She began pacing, her walking shoes squeaking on the linoleum floor with every step she took. "How could I be so stupid? So heartless? Bringing him here would be like taking a burn victim to a bonfire, for heaven's sake."

"Now, it's not quite like that…"

"Yes, it is. He's an orphan. He lost his mother not that long ago, and his father might as well be dead. And what do I do? Take him to see a bunch of orphaned animals. Then, to make it worse, I tell him all about how they'll be let loose. 'Abandoned,' I think is what he called it."

"Hey, you couldn't have known he'd take it that way. We'll talk to him, make sure he knows that no one is going to abandon him."

"It was still insensitive. I should have known better."

"News flash, princess. You can't always have all the answers, or get it all right. Not when it comes to kids. Yeah, you screwed up. You'll fix it. And then probably do something else to mess up, and then fix that. It's how the whole thing works."

She stopped pacing just a foot away from him and stared at him. She was close enough that he could smell the scent of whatever fancy shampoo she used, something girly.

"You know, I'm not sure if I want to thank you or smack you."

He shrugged a shoulder. "I'm not trying to make you feel better, just telling you the truth."

"Which is that I screwed up, but it's not a big deal because I'll probably do it again?"

"Something like that, yeah."

She cocked her head, as if trying to judge if he was serious. Which he was. If he'd learned anything since his girls were born, it was that it was impossible to predict what would set them off. And that making mistakes was par for the course. That they were doing okay was more a statement about their resilience than his own parenting skills.

"Fine. But can we go get him now?"

"Sure, but don't push him, okay? He's a guy, and he's going to feel dumb about crying. Don't make it worse by fussing over him too much."

"Isn't he a little young to be worried about all that macho stuff?"

"Nope. Boys his age want to be seen as fearless. I'm not saying you can't talk to him about it, but just let him take the lead, okay?"

"Fine, let's just go." Moving past him she went out the same door Kevin had used.

Tyler followed her onto a mulch path that ran alongside the building and out toward what must be the animal enclosures. To the left was an enclosed space similar to a barn. To the right were open pens ringed with chain-link fencing. At the farthest one, with his back to them, was Kevin.

Dani's footsteps quickened, but at least she didn't run up and hug the kid. Instead, she positioned herself next to him, looking into the enclosure. Tyler joined her, flanking Kevin's other side. For a minute the three of them just stood there, watching what seemed to be a very relaxed, very large panther grooming itself in the sun.

Dani spoke first. "That's Simba, the panther I was telling you about. You'd never know it now, but he used to be really nervous—in fact, he was terrified of strangers. My sister Mollie's done a lot of work with him to help him build up his confidence."

Kevin blinked in surprise. "The panther was scared of people? Doesn't he know he could just eat them if he wanted?"

"I guess not." Dani shrugged. "He used to be a pet, sort of. A mean man kept him locked up all the time in a small cage, and it wasn't very nice. When he was rescued and brought here, he didn't know if the new people he met were going to be mean to him, like the place he came from. It took time, and lots of people being nice to him, before he was able to relax and enjoy his new home."

Tyler watched Kevin take that in, no doubt relating it to his own experience moving from foster home to foster home. "That makes sense. I'm glad the people here are nice to him."

"Me, too." Relief flooded Dani's face. "Now, do you want to see the rest of the animals? Some of them have had hard times, like Simba, so if that makes you sad, we could do something else." She glanced over at Tyler and smiled. "Like go get ice cream or something."

Kevin looked at Simba for another minute before speaking, his voice so soft Tyler could barely hear it. "Are the other animals happy now?"

She smiled. "Yeah, buddy, they are."

"Okay, I'd like to see them then. I like happy endings."

After seeing all the other animals, which were thankfully deemed happy by Kevin, they ended up at the ice-cream parlor after all. It wasn't like she could say no, not after how badly she'd messed up earlier. She'd half expected Tyler to veto the idea, but he'd readily agreed and had even insisted on treating them all. Every time she thought she'd started to figure him out, he'd change things up on her.

In court he'd been cold and distant, almost clinical in his description of what had happened. In the park he'd been patient but firm in his convictions. At the rehab center he'd surprised her by letting her take the lead while he mostly observed. And now he was chatting casually with Kevin, each arguing the merits of their preferred ice-cream flavor. Dani hadn't been able to get a word in edgewise. Which was fine; it was good that they were starting to bond. And Kevin was smiling, which was awesome. She had a feeling she'd feel guilty about the incident with the orphaned possum for a long time, but he seemed none the worse for it.

The real reason she couldn't seem to relax had nothing to do with Kevin and everything to do with the man sitting across from him, extolling the virtues of mint chocolate-chip ice cream. Not that he was doing anything wrong. He was just…confusing. She couldn't get a read on him, and that was making her crazy. As a lawyer she had taught herself to be good at reading faces, at knowing what people were thinking even when they weren't saying it and be able to grasp what was going on inside someone's head. But with Tyler, she was at a loss. And damn if it didn't make her want to spend more time with him, if only to satisfy her own curiosity.

And curiosity was all it was. No way was she ready to date. On her good days she felt like she'd made a lot of progress since she'd come home, but she couldn't kid herself: she was gun-shy and with good reason. Besides, he wasn't her type. She tended to date lawyers and bankers, men who wore suits and read the stock report. She wasn't a snob; she just found that she enjoyed dating men who had similar goals and interests, ambitious men who understood her own drive and dedication to her career. Tyler Jackson was a small-town shopkeeper and single dad who drove a minivan, of all things. So if she couldn't take her eyes off of him, it was just because she was trying to figure him out. That's all.

Kevin stood up abruptly, nearly knocking his soda

over in the process. She grabbed the cup as he waved at someone behind her. Turning, she spotted his foster parents walking through the door. She'd called earlier and arranged for them to pick up the boy here. Tyler followed her gaze and then stood, offering his seat to a tired-looking Mrs. Cunningham.

"You must be the Cunninghams. I'm Tyler. Can I get you anything? A cold drink, or some ice cream?"

"No, thank you, but we won't be staying. I've got dinner to make still, and need to be getting home. I would have stayed in the car, but I wanted to thank you personally, and apologize on behalf of Kevin for what he did. My husband and I were so upset when we found out. I still don't know what got into him…"

"Now, Nora, let's not get into it again. What's done is done. If Mr. Jackson here can see past things, I suppose we can, too." He held out a grizzled, arthritic hand to Tyler. "I'm Tom Cunningham. Nora and I appreciate the time you're spending with Kevin. We adore him, but two old people like us aren't much fun, I'm afraid." He turned to Kevin. "Ready to go?"

"Yes, sir." He shoved the last bite of his chocolate-waffle cone in his mouth and swallowed. "'Bye, Dani. 'Bye, Tyler. See you next week?"

Tyler nodded. "You bet."

"And can Dani come again?"

Uh-oh. That hadn't been part of the plan. She looked at Tyler, who nodded good-naturedly. "Um, sure, I guess. If that's what you want."

"Cool. 'Bye!"

Dani sighed, and sank back into her chair. "Well, that was quite the day. Sorry about him inviting me along for next time. I didn't know he was going to do that."

Tyler sat beside her and took a sip of his drink. "It's fine. Having his energy level back up can only be a good thing."

"Good point." She sobered. "Speaking of which, I'm starting to worry he's too much for the Cunninghams. They've done foster care for a long time, but they look more tired than I remember. More…well, old. I'm not sure how much longer they're going to be able to do this."

Tyler frowned. "I don't know what they were like before, but given how energetic kids Kevin's age are, I understand what you mean. I'd hate for him to have to move to yet another foster home, but it might be inevitable."

Dani's stomach clenched, the ice cream that had seemed such a good idea earlier now a cold weight in her gut. "I just want to make things easier for him, you know? But I have no idea how—I couldn't even schedule an outing without upsetting him."

Tyler reached across the table, laying his hand on hers. "Hey, don't beat yourself up. You were trying, and he knows that. That's what counts. That's what he needs, people that care enough to try."

Her hand tingled, a warm feeling where his skin touched hers. Tugging it back, she fisted her hands in her lap. "I just wish I could do more, something to really help him."

"Well, if you mean that, you could talk to his case worker about getting him some counseling. A therapist could help him work through his feelings about his mom, and help him with any transitions that might come up."

Hell, why hadn't she thought of that? "You're right. I'll call her as soon as I get home, and see what she can set up. I'll drive him myself to the appointments if need be. Thanks. I'll call you and let you know how it turns out." Finally, she had something concrete to do. Just knowing she had a plan chased away a bit of the restlessness that had been plaguing her. Grabbing her purse, she started for the door, feeling more confident than she had since this whole thing started. Funny how the man she'd been convinced was ruining Kevin's life just a few days ago was the one giving her an insight into how to help him. Remembering how she'd treated him at the park that day, she felt her cheeks heat. She never had apologized for that. She stopped, her hand on the door, and turned back to him.

"Listen, about the other day… I'm sorry if I jumped to conclusions about you. I just—"

"You just wanted to protect Kevin. I get that." He smiled. "I don't want to be your enemy, Dani. I just want to do what's right."

"I believe you." Which was somehow sexier than a power suit or a fast car. Who'd have guessed?

Chapter Three

Dani knocked on the door of the Cunninghams' small but well-built home and waited. The couple had called earlier, asking to meet, and she'd skipped lunch in order to stop by. The house itself was in one of Paradise's older neighborhoods, built in an old Florida style with stucco exteriors and large windows to take advantage of the sea breeze. Most had well-kept yards, but a few weeds were beginning to take over the flower bed around the Cunninghams' mailbox, and the paint was peeling on the door. Small things, but it made her wonder again about their health.

Muffled footsteps from inside were followed by the creak of the door opening. "Dani, thank you for coming so quickly." Mrs. Cunningham waved her in, and then led her into the kitchen. "Have a seat and I'll get us some iced tea."

Dani sat at a scarred wooden table, where a bowl of fresh-cut gardenia blossoms floated in water. "Gardenias are my favorite flower. My parents have a big bush that grows right under my old bedroom window. I used to love falling asleep with that smell in the air."

"They do make the house smell good, don't they? Kevin picked those for me yesterday. He's such a sweet boy." She set down a full glass of amber tea, condensation already forming on the side. "Full of energy, though. The poor bush looks half-scalped now." She sat, sighing as she did so. "But his heart is in the right place, I think."

"I agree. But after a day with him yesterday, I know what you mean. I imagine that's normal, though, for a boy his age."

"Oh, it is. We've had fifteen different foster children over the years, plus our own kids, of course, and they all have more energy than sense at times. Kevin's no different. The problem isn't Kevin, it's us." She folded her hands in front of her, and grimaced. "The truth of the matter is, I'm getting old. No, I am old. And so is my husband, even if he won't admit it. We've both got some health issues, nothing too serious, but I'm probably going to need a knee replacement sooner rather than later. And Tom's blood pressure is getting harder to control. The doctor says he has to start taking it easy or he's going to end up having a heart attack one day."

Hearing her suspicions stated out loud made the sweet tea sour in her mouth. "I'm so sorry. Is there something I can do?"

The older woman nodded, her tightly permed grey hair barely budging at the movement. "Not for us, but for Kevin. The social worker said you're his advocate, and I figured you should be the first to know. We're going to have to give up fostering. My daughter has found us a nice one-bedroom apartment in one of those assisted-living facilities, where I can get some extra help when I have my surgery, and Tom won't have to do yard work anymore. It's the right thing for us, but Kevin's going to take it hard."

That was an understatement. "I understand. I don't know what I can do, but I'll try to make things easier for him. Has he been to the therapist yet? She should know, too." Dani had spoken with the caseworker just a few days ago about arranging some counseling, but hadn't heard anything further. Maybe she should have followed up sooner, but her own workload had kept her busy since then.

"He has an appointment tomorrow after school with someone the social worker recommended. Thank you, by the way, for suggesting it. I should have thought of it myself, but lately it's been all I can do to keep track of my own doctor visits."

"I'm glad they were able to find someone for him. You'll want to tell whoever he sees about this, so they can help him deal with it. They have the training for this kind of thing."

"Of course, and we will. But Kevin's really taken with you. He talks about you all the time. I think he looks up to you, what with being a lawyer and having that fancy car. He'll get whatever counseling he needs, but he's going to need a friend, too. And I'd just feel better about this whole thing if I knew you'd be keeping an eye on him." She quickly wiped a tear from the corner of her eye. "I don't mind telling you that I feel sick about this. If it was just me, I'd manage. But Tom's had some chest pains, and—"

"And you have to take care of yourselves. You can't risk your health… What would happen to Kevin then? He'd still have to move to a new family, and he'd be worried sick about you. No, you have to follow the doctor's orders. Kevin will be okay." She tried to project confidence, but worry was already worming its way through her mind. How would Kevin handle yet another move? Would he act out again? He was still on probation; he couldn't afford to make any more mistakes. And would the new family support him, or would he be labeled a troublemaker and a thief? Mind whirling, she stood to go. She'd get back to the office, make some calls and talk to his social worker. If there was a way to make this easier on him, she'd do it. Not just because it was her job as his guardian *ad litem*, but also because she wasn't going to be able to sleep at night if she didn't.

Owning a toy store didn't sound like a physical job, but when crates of wooden blocks and assorted toys needed to be carried around it sure felt like one. Grunting, Tyler lifted the last box of new inventory, feeling his biceps burn. Or course, he could have opened the big box in the storeroom and then carried the individual packages of blocks to the shelf one at a time, but that would have taken forever. And he still had the ego of a twenty-year-old, if not the back of one. Pushing thirty and some days it felt like fifty, but the work got done and that's what mattered.

Lugging the load to the display shelves, he heard the bell signaling a customer had come in. Usually they were slow between lunch and when school got out, which was why he'd chosen to start stocking the shelves. Now he'd have to stop and hope he could get back to it before he was inundated with elementary-school kids looking to spend their allowance. Oh, well, that's how it went some days.

"I'll be right there." He set down the box with a sigh, then made his way to the sales desk. Waiting for him, her fingers nervously tapping out a rhythm on the counter, was Dani. He hadn't seen her since Saturday, and hadn't expected to until the next outing with Kevin. Not that he minded the unexpected visit. A beautiful woman was welcome anytime, and she was looking especially attractive today. A green blouse with a scoop neck showed just a hint of cleavage and was tucked neatly into a charcoal pencil skirt that skimmed her hips and ended just above the knee. Black, lethal-looking spiked heels completed the outfit. Sexy but professional, she had him drooling like a kid at the candy counter.

Clearing his throat, he stepped behind the counter in hopes of hiding his sudden surge of arousal. "Hi, Dani. Can I help you find something?"

"Not unless you have a fairy wand stashed somewhere. The real kind that I can use to fix all of Kevin's problems."

"Fresh out, I'm afraid." He searched her face, seeing sadness in the chocolate depths of her eyes. She'd bitten off most of her lipstick, too, a nervous habit he'd noticed the other day. Something was definitely up. "What's going on with Kevin? Did he get in more trouble?"

"No, of course not!" She shoved a piece of hair back

with one hand, only to have it swing forward again. "I told you, he's a good kid. But I just talked to the Cunninghams, and they're having some health problems. In fact, they're moving into an assisted-living facility. Soon."

He was pretty sure he knew the answer, but he asked anyway. "And where does that leave Kevin?"

"I don't know—in some other foster home, or even the group home over on the mainland. No one knows yet. I talked to his social worker on the way here, and she said it could take a while to find an available foster family. They just have too many kids and not enough people willing to take them in."

"Man, that's rough. Kevin really liked the Cunninghams, from what I can tell."

She nodded. "He did. They don't have a lot of energy, but they're kind to him. I get the feeling not everywhere has been so nice. I just wish I knew what to do about it."

"I don't think there is anything you can do, other than keep the lines of communication open. I'll do the same. Other than that, it's up to fate."

Her eyes snapped with fire. "I don't believe in leaving things up to fate. There has to be something we can do." She paced, her heels making a clacking noise on the tiled floor. "Maybe you could try to get the charges dropped against him."

"That's not going to change anything, and besides, it's too late. I couldn't if I wanted to. Which I don't."

Dani's mouth dropped open, but before she could launch into a new argument he continued, "Because he needs to know that his actions have consequences. Now, when he's still young enough to learn from them.

Otherwise he could end up thinking he can get away with stuff like this, and once he's eighteen he'd face real jail time. He could mess up his life forever. Better he have probation now and change his ways than end up in jail a few years from now."

"I don't think that's likely to happen."

"Maybe not, but I'm not willing to chance it. I know how easy it is to get caught up in the wrong crowd, making bad decisions. Especially now that he's going to be facing even more upheaval. Trust me. Probation, the mentorship program—those aren't the problems. They're the best way to help him until the real problem can be addressed."

"And I suppose you have an answer to that, too?"

"Sure. He needs a home, a real home. We can try to help him, the counselors can, the social workers. But until he gets a home of his own he's going to be fighting an uphill battle."

Dani pursed her lips, her eyes distant as she appeared to think over his answer. Then she nodded, a smile breaking out over her face, her confidence back in spades. "You're right."

"I am?" He thought he was, but he hadn't expected her to sound so sure of it.

"Yup. He needs a family. So I'll give him one. I'll foster him myself."

"You're going to what?" Tyler's mouth dropped open, making him look a bit like one of the marionettes hanging slack-jawed on the display behind him.

"Foster him." She chewed her lip, thinking quickly. "I guess that would be the first step. You said it yourself—he needs a real home, stability."

"You're insane."

"I am not." Okay, so it was a bit impulsive, but there was no logical reason she couldn't do this. "I've got a steady job, a two-bedroom apartment, and he likes me."

Tyler laughed, a harsh, cynical sound. "And you think that's all it takes to be a parent? An extra bedroom and a source of income?"

"No, but it's a start." She'd thought he'd be supportive, excited even, at the prospect of Kevin getting out of foster care. Obviously she'd misjudged him. "Never mind. I shouldn't have come here. Obviously you don't care what happens to him. Why should you? He's just some punk kid who broke the law." Anger and disappointment washed over her, threatening to coalesce into tears. And she never cried. Certainly not in public. Turning for the door, she bit her lip and reminded herself that Tyler's opinion meant nothing to her. Why she kept trusting men when they kept letting her down, she had no idea. When it came to the opposite sex, her judgment sucked.

A hand on her arm spun her back, Tyler's face only inches from hers. "That's what you've got wrong. I do care, and that's why I think this is a bad idea. You have no idea what you are getting into, taking in a kid like Kevin. It's not going to be fun and games. It's going to be hard and ugly. And when it gets to be too much you'll leave him, and he'll be worse off than before. So, sorry if I'm not going to be your biggest cheerleader when you treat fostering a child with the same amount of thought as an impulse purchase at the mall. He's a human being, not a designer purse you can replace next season."

She clutched her purse and narrowed her eyes. "I know that. And I have no intention of replacing him, or whatever it is you're implying. I don't quit, ever. If I start something, I finish it."

"You do know Kevin isn't a thing, or a task to be accomplished—he's a person."

"Of course I do." Wasn't that the whole reason she was doing this? To help someone who couldn't help himself?

"For his sake, I hope so."

"You have no idea who I am, or what I'm capable of." She'd meant what she said: she wasn't a quitter. At least she hadn't been, until her life got turned upside down. In her own mind, she needed to still be the strong woman she'd always prided herself on being.

"I know that trying to parent a troubled kid isn't in the same league as studying for entrance exams or getting through law school. Like I said, you have no idea what you are getting into."

Frustration and something else fired through her. "Well then, why don't you help me? If you're such an expert, you can make sure I get it right."

"Whoa, slow down. I'm not getting involved. This is your idea, not mine. I don't want any part of this crazy plan."

"All talk, no action, huh?"

He glared. "I'm just being realistic."

She glared right back. She'd had plenty of practice handling alpha males in court and had no intention of letting this one intimidate her. "Realistic or cynical?"

A flash of pain illuminated his eyes before his expression hardened, locking out any trace of emotion. "In my experience it's the same thing. Crap happens, and all the good intentions in the world can't change that."

"Of course not. But surely that's a good place to start." She'd been let down when people who should have helped had turned a blind eye. She wouldn't do that to Kevin.

He stayed silent, as if weighing her words, before finally shrugging in half-hearted acceptance. "Maybe. But I'm serious—you can't just go upending his life on a whim. You have to be sure. Being a single parent is the hardest thing there is, and that's true even when it's your biological child."

She counted to ten silently. He wasn't trying to make her mad, and he had some good points. But just because it was hard didn't mean it wasn't the right decision. Surely he could understand that. Taking a deep breath, she tried again. "I believe you. I can't imagine what you or any single parent goes through. And I know this will be hard. But if I can do it, if I can keep him from going into a group home, and make things easier for him, then I should at least try." She knew what it was like, to feel insignificant, as if you were at the mercy of a system you had no hope of changing. No one had stood up for her, but she could be there for Kevin. Her throat tightened with emotion. "Tyler, I can't just watch his life be disrupted again, and not do anything about it. I can't."

Tense silence met her plea, and then he let out a labored sigh. "Damn it. You don't make anything easy, do you?"

"Easy doesn't mean right." She'd taken the easy way out by coming home, and it kept her up at night. She wasn't going to make the same mistake again.

"No, I guess it doesn't. Fine, then, let's say you decide to do this. What do you have to do to be a foster parent?"

"I don't know. Yet." She pulled out her phone and did an internet search for "Palmetto County foster parent" and found the page for the Department of Children and Families. Scanning quickly, she found a section about emergency and temporary placements. "It looks like I might be able to get clearance more quickly, given that I already have a relationship with him. And I've been through most of the background checks as part of the guardian *ad litem* program. But I'll call his social worker and see what she says. I want to have things in place before he leaves the Cunninghams." She looked up at him. "I'll make this work. I won't let him go to a group home. I won't let him down." There was nothing worse than having the people you trusted turn their backs on you. She'd learned that lesson too well, and part of her would never be the same. If she could protect whatever hope Kevin had left, whatever belief he had in good winning out over evil, she would.

Tyler shook his head. "What scares me is, I'm starting to believe it. Now go. Make it happen before I come to my senses and try to talk you out of it."

"Thanks!" Impulsively she leaned in and hugged him, then froze, expecting the panic to set in. Instead, she felt a pulse of lightning shoot through her, lighting up nerves that had lain dormant so long she'd forgotten what they were for. Heat and confusion filled her head, leaving her dizzy as she pulled back. "I've got to go…call the social worker."

Tyler nodded, stepping away from her. "And I've got inventory to unpack. But, Dani?"

"Yes?" Her pulse sped. Had she overstepped with the hug? Had he read something in to it?

"Never mind. Just…good luck."

Chapter Four

Dani spent the car ride back to her office purposely not thinking about the hug. Or about the way her body had reacted. Or about how good he had felt. Heck, he'd even smelled good. But she wasn't thinking about that. It was inappropriate, with him being Kevin's mentor and her being his guardian *ad litem*. Instead, she should just focus on the fact that she hadn't freaked out. That was a major breakthrough, and a sign that the therapist she'd been seeing was worth the time and stress of driving to the mainland every other week. Seeing one of the few therapists in Paradise was out of the question; inevitably someone would have seen her coming or going into the office and asked questions she didn't want to answer. Or worse, would have asked her family about it, and she didn't want them to know anything about what had happened. She was an adult, and it was her issue to handle. And if her reaction to Tyler was any indication, she was making progress.

But a fleeting attraction, as heartening as it was, wasn't an excuse to get sidetracked. Right now she needed to focus on Kevin, and his situation. Which meant as soon as she got to her desk she needed to call his social worker. Pulling into the small parking lot, she spied several unfamiliar cars. Good, that meant her parents would be busy and wouldn't want to chat about where she'd been or what she was up to. She'd fill them in on the Kevin situation once she had more information. After Tyler's initial reaction, she didn't want to risk any more negativity.

Once inside she blinked at the cool dimness, letting her eyes adjust from the bright tropical sun outside. Her mom, on the phone as always, waved hello, then pointed at her father's office. Dani shook her head; she didn't have time to schmooze a client right now. It wasn't like her father needed her legal advice; he just liked showing off his eldest daughter to clients, taking pleasure in promoting the firm as a family affair. Cute, but today wasn't the day for it.

She had almost made it to her own office when she heard a door open behind her. Crap. She was caught.

"Dani, there you are! I've got someone here I want you to meet."

She turned slowly, forcing a smile to her face. Standing next to her father was a man about her own age, dressed in the Florida version of country-club casual: a golf shirt, neatly pressed khakis and boat shoes. Flashing her a brilliant smile that showcased perfect teeth, he stepped toward her, hand outstretched. "Hello, Dani. Your father's told me a lot about you."

He stepped into her space, and without thinking she stepped backward, her foot hitting the closed door of her office. Sweat trickled between her breasts. Damn it, and here she'd been congratulating herself on making progress with her fears. Clamping down on the adrenaline thrumming through her body, she shook his hand and reminded herself her father was in the room; she was totally safe. He'd done nothing wrong, other than to move in a bit too quickly, and a bit too close. But that was typical with alpha males, especially in the business world. "Nice to meet you, um—"

"Sorry, Richard. Richard Thompson. Your father's helping me with a trust I'm setting up."

"That's great." Unable to stand it any longer, she eased around him, moving into the center of the room, where she had space to breathe and an open view of the front door.

"Richard is setting up a charitable trust, as a matter of fact. Very praiseworthy for a single man his age, I have to say."

The emphasis her father put on the word *single* sent a new kind of fear through her. Was her father playing matchmaker? Seriously?

"Your father told me about your work with the guardian *ad litem* program. It seems we share a common interest in philanthropy. Maybe we could have dinner sometime, and see what else we have in common."

Well, at least he didn't beat around the bush. It was definitely a setup. Too bad the offer held as much interest as an emergency root canal. "Sounds lovely, but I'm afraid I'm a bit swamped at the moment. In fact, I'm late for a phone meeting right now. If you'll excuse me…" She moved purposefully back toward her office, forcing him to move out of the way.

"Of course." Mr. Charitable Trust graciously nodded and moved back to her father, who looked puzzled by her behavior, but was too polite to say anything. Meanwhile her mother had finally gotten off the phone and was watching the entire scene like it was her favorite telenovela. So much for keeping business business.

Closing the door behind her, she locked it for good measure, and then leaned heavily against the cool wood, waiting for her breathing to return to normal.

She'd definitely panicked out there, but she'd stayed in control, and she'd handled it. Her therapist would be proud.

It was strange, though, how different her reaction was to Tyler. Of course, she knew Tyler. He wasn't a stranger. And she'd initiated the contact. That was probably why.

Thinking of the encounter with Tyler reminded her of Kevin, and the reason she'd rushed back to the office so quickly. Moving to her desk, she grabbed a fresh legal pad and picked up the phone.

"Hi, this is Dani Post. May I speak to Elaine, please? Tell her it's about Kevin. I think I've found a foster home for him."

Tyler threw his energy into unpacking the boxes of wooden blocks that he'd started to unload earlier, hoping to quiet his mind with some good old physical labor. But no matter how fast or how hard he worked, he couldn't get Dani off of his mind. She was infuriating, that was for sure. So sure she knew what was right, and full of self-righteousness. But as annoying as she could be, that wasn't what was bothering him. No, it wasn't her words or her attitude haunting him; it was the way she'd felt in his arms. One impulsive hug shouldn't have gotten under his skin, into his head. But it had.

His body had reacted immediately, which on its own wasn't that surprising. She was a beautiful woman, sexy in a high-class, dressed-up kind of way. But it wasn't just a moment of lust that had him still thinking about her, wondering if she'd worked things out with the social worker, wondering what she did for fun or what her favorite way to relax was. That was…interest. And he couldn't afford to be interested in a woman.

As if to reinforce that thought, the front bell rang out, followed by twin voices calling, "Daddy!" Setting down a box of brightly colored building blocks, he scooped one girl up in each arm. They were in full-day kindergarten now, but as far as he was concerned they were still his little girls. Even if they were big enough to ride the bus and have homework.

"Hey, monsters. How was school?"

"Great!"

"Boring."

He laughed and set them down. For twins, they sure had a hard time agreeing on anything. "All right, Adelaide first. What was great?" Maybe if he focused on the positive first, Amy would, too.

"We got to play kickball in gym class today, and I kicked the ball so hard it went a mile!"

"No, it didn't go a mile. A mile is really, really far." Amy frowned in annoyance. "You just kicked it to the edge of the field."

Adelaide tossed her head, pigtails flying. "You're just jealous because you struck out."

"I am not. It's a stupid game, anyway." Amy was a bookworm who would much rather read than play sports. It wasn't that she wasn't as talented or athletic as her sister; she just truly didn't see the point of sports.

"Maybe they'll play something you like better to-morrow. In the meantime, I picked up some muffins for you at the Sandcastle Bakery. They're in the break room if you're hungry."

"Yes!"

"Yes!"

Finally in agreement about something, they blew past him, their small feet echoing on the tile floor. Following at a saner pace he found them seated at the child-size table he'd made for them, all grins and crumbs. The entire space had been designed with them in mind. He'd purchased the toy store when Jennifer was pregnant, and the idea had been that the shop would be a place where the whole family was welcome. Initially that had meant high chairs and playpens, but now the room held a reading nook with beanbag chairs and a small bookshelf, a play area complete with an indoor tent and the table where they could eat, draw or do homework. There was also a couch and a kitch-enette: basically all the comforts of home. After Jen-nifer's death the girls had spent even more time here, preferring to be close to their father than at the house with a babysitter. Maybe it was selfish of him but in his grief he'd needed them, too. So they worked out a routine where they spent the afternoons together at the shop, and he hired someone to close up so they could go home and have dinner together.

So far it was working out well. Of course, what kid wouldn't want to spend their days in a toy store? Not to mention, as cute as the girls were, every customer ended up spending as much time with them as they did shopping. His mascots, he called them, and they'd worked out a pretty good routine together. Which was why he wasn't going to risk what they'd built by even thinking about adding a romance into it. These two girls were more than enough female for him. They were his whole life, and he'd make any sacrifice to make sure they grew up secure and happy.

Amy finished her muffin first, and looked up at him. "Are we going to get our kitten today?"

His heart sunk. "No, not today. I've got to finish unloading the rest of the new stock today, and then it will be time for dinner and bed."

Adelaide pouted. "You said we could get a kitty."

"I know I did. And we will."

"When?" Leave it to the more serious Amy to want to nail down the details.

"I don't know," he answered truthfully. "Soon. Whenever I can get a break here at the shop." He did want to get them a kitten; the responsibility of a pet was good for kids. And they'd been asking forever. But the tiny town animal shelter was only open a few days a week, and their hours happened to coincide with the hours of his own shop, making the logistics of getting said kitten more difficult than he'd planned. But he'd find a way to work it out. "Soon."

"That's what you said last week." Adelaide's voice ventured close to whining, but he didn't have the heart to correct her. He'd let them down, and they had every right to be upset.

He thought of Dani, and her decision to foster, to be a single parent. He'd meant it when he'd wished her good luck. Not because he doubted her sincerity or her ability. But because being a parent was so darned hard. And as the kitten fiasco showed, even after all this time he was still finding new ways to mess things up.

"So, what's the big emergency?" Mollie, Dani's sister, asked as she pushed by her carrying two canvas grocery bags. "Whatever it is, I think I've got us covered—three kinds of ice cream, two kinds of chips, dip and a bottle of red wine. Noah picked out the wine, so it's some brand I've never heard of but it's probably amazing."

Mollie's husband, Noah, was a famous metal sculptor and had run in some very well-to-do crowds before deciding he preferred the slower pace of small-town life. He definitely knew more about upscale wine than the rest of them. "I'm sure it will be great. Although I'm not sure fancy wine goes with chips and dip and ice cream."

Mollie rolled her eyes. "Wine goes with everything. Especially when there's a crisis. Which you still haven't told me about."

Dani ripped open a bag of salt-and-vinegar chips and grabbed a handful. "It's not a crisis, exactly. And I'd rather just tell the whole thing once, when everyone gets here."

"Fine, be that way." Mollie uncorked the wine bottle and poured two glasses. "Who all is coming?"

Taking one of the glasses, Dani took a tentative sip of the ruby-colored liquid. "Wow, that is good." She took another, larger sip. "Sam's working late, but said she'd get here as soon as she could." Sam Finley and

Dani had become friends soon after Sam moved to Paradise to take a job with the Florida Fish and Wildlife Commission. Now married to Dylan, the director at the wildlife refuge, she was a regular attendee at any girls' night activities. "Jillian is definitely coming, and Cassie said she would, too, as long as Alex makes it home in time to watch the kids."

As if on cue, the doorbell rang, and the next few minutes were a crush of hugs, laughter and good-natured ribbing as the remaining women arrived, each bearing food to contribute to the night. Cassie had brought pizza, Jillian had homemade brownies and Sam, who had managed to finish up quicker than planned, had stopped at a convenience store to grab some bottles of soda.

"Sorry, it was all I had time for," she offered apologetically, unloading her bag onto the counter with the rest of the food.

Dani rolled her eyes as she passed out paper plates for the pizza. "Please, lady. You know we don't care if you bring anything. We're just glad you came."

"I've got a ton of paperwork to finish up later, but I figure the paperwork can wait. Friends can't." She took a bite of pepperoni pizza and moaned in appreciation. "Besides, I was starving."

"Me, too." Jillian filled her plate and headed for the small dining area. "I swear, I'm twice as hungry with this pregnancy as the last one. I'm going to look full-term by the time I'm out of the first trimester." A mother of one, Jillian had recently announced her second pregnancy.

"You know," Cassie mused, filling her own plate, "it could be twins. Maybe you're eating for three."

Jillian's face blanched. "You don't really think so, do you?"

"No, probably not," Cassie assured her. "But it does happen. When is your first ultrasound?"

"Not for another few weeks. But enough about me and how fat I'm getting. What's going on, Dani? Why the urgent meeting?"

"Yeah, spill it," Mollie agreed. "What's going on? Guy problems?"

"I guess you could say that, but the guy in question is about four feet tall and only nine years old."

Mollie's mouth dropped open, her pizza forgotten. "Um, come again?"

A smile crept over Dani's face. It wasn't often she was able to shock her sister. "He's one of my guardian *ad litem* cases."

Quickly she filled them in, starting with the court case and finishing with the retirement of his foster parents and her idea of stepping into their place.

"So wait, you're going to adopt him?" Cassie's eyes widened. "I didn't know you were even interested in starting a family."

"I wasn't, not until I met Kevin. And I'd be fostering him, to start with. There's a whole process I have to go through. Maybe I'm crazy to even be thinking about it."

"No, you aren't. You're amazing." Jillian's voice trembled with emotion. "Remember, I grew up in the foster system, and what you are thinking about doing is incredible. I got lucky in a few homes, but most of them were just better than homelessness. Kevin would be lucky to have someone like you in his life."

"But does being in his life have to mean fostering him? You're already involved, as his guardian *ad litem*. Are you sure you're ready for more than that?"

Cassie's words echoed Dani's own doubts. "Honestly, I don't know. Were you ready to be a mom when you had Emma?"

Cassie took a big swallow of wine. "No, not in the least. But I didn't really have much of a choice. You do." She set down her glass, and met Dani's gaze. "I'm not saying you shouldn't do it. Honestly, you're way more mature than I was when I became a mom. But being a single parent is hard, the hardest thing there is. I just want to be sure you know what you're getting into."

"I don't know. There's something to be said for just being thrown into parenthood," Mollie interjected. "When Noah and I fell in love, he didn't even know he had a son. But once he found out, I had to accept that being with Noah meant taking on his child. There really wasn't time to prepare, or consider what that meant. I just knew I didn't want to lose the man I loved. And honestly, as much as I never thought I would, I love that baby more than life itself." She shrugged. "Sometimes you just have to follow your heart."

No doubt that advice had worked out just fine for her sister. But Mollie always had been the impulsive one. She knew how to make any situation work for her. Dani was the one that made a plan and followed it, step by step. Was she brave enough to toss all that aside?

But if she didn't, could she live with herself, knowing she could have helped, but was too scared to try? She'd let fear control her decisions once. Was she willing to do that again?

"Maybe that's my problem. My heart is just as confused at the rest of me."

"Well, if you do end up doing this, you know we'll support you." The others nodded at Jillian's words. "Single parent or not, you won't be in this on your own."

Tears stung Dani's eyes. "Thanks, guys. I'll hold you to that, because I have a feeling I'm going to need all the help I can get."

Chapter Five

Tyler stood on Dani's doorstep, listening to the doorbell ringing, wondering if he'd made a big mistake. He glanced again at the stack of parenting books in his hands. Was it weird for a guy to have a bunch of parenting books? Somehow, what had seemed perfectly normal when he'd initially thought of it now seemed too forward, not to mention potentially less than masculine. But the truth was, although it had only been ten days since they'd talked, he'd wanted an excuse to see her again, and this was as good a reason as any.

He heard a dead bolt turn, and then the door opened, revealing a much more casual Dani than he'd seen before. Wearing paint-splattered cutoffs that showed off what seemed like miles of toned legs, a ragged T-shirt with the sleeves cut off and a bandana over her mussed hair, she was the definition of a hot mess. And still the sexiest thing he'd ever seen.

"Tyler? What's going on? Is it something with Kevin?"

"No, he's fine." He held up the books as an offering. "I just thought I'd drop these off. I got your message that things were moving forward with the foster approval, and I thought you might find them helpful."

One eyebrow lifted, but she nodded. "Um, okay." Backing up, her bare feet slapping against the tile, she motioned him in. "Excuse the mess. I'm trying to get everything ready before Kevin moves in, and it's taking a lot longer than I thought it would."

What looked like office furniture was shoved into every available space in the living room, and painting supplies took up the breakfast bar. Legal files littered the coffee table, along with a box from the local bakery and a half-full mug of coffee. On the floor were flat pack boxes of furniture, and a mattress was leaning precariously against the couch. Looking around, he didn't see an empty spot anywhere. "So, where would you like me to put these?"

She threw up her hands. "Honestly, anywhere you can find a space. The kitchen is still kind of in one piece, so that's probably your best bet. Once I finish painting I can move the new furniture in and put the old in storage. Until then, I'm trying to embrace the chaos."

"So I see." He followed her into the small, eat-in kitchen and found a clear spot on the counter to set the books down.

Dani ran a finger over the spines, then looked up in surprise. "These are yours?"

"Yeah." He shoved his hands into pockets. "After Jennifer died, I needed all the help I could get. I thought maybe they would help you get up to speed, since all this is happening so fast. If you're not interested, I can donate them to the library or something."

"No! I want them. I just was a bit surprised—"

"That a Neanderthal like me could read?"

She rolled her eyes. "Nothing that awful. I guess you seem so confident that it's hard to imagine you buying self-help books of any kind."

Confident? That he could live with. "When it comes to parenting, no one is that confident, trust me." He tapped on the top book. "This one is specifically about helping kids who have been through trauma. You might want to start there."

"Thanks." She put her hands on her hips and looked around. "Although when I'm going to have the time to read anything, I'm not sure. There's so much to do before the caseworker comes out to do the home inspection and everything is happening faster than I thought it would."

"Want some help?"

She blinked. "Are you offering?"

Was he? "Sure, the girls are at my parents' for the day, so I've got some time to kill. And I'm pretty good with a paint roller."

"Seriously?" She smiled, and he found himself thinking he'd do a hell of a lot more than paint a room to get her to smile at him again. "You're a lifesaver. My sister's supposed to be helping, but she was doing a photo shoot first thing this morning and she has a tendency to get sucked into her work and forget everything else. And I'll admit, I'm a bit intimidated by all the painting stuff. I watched some videos online, but I've never actually done any of this before."

"Don't worry. It's not that complicated. If you show me what supplies you have, we'll get started." He began to walk out of the kitchen, only to be stopped by Dani's hand on his arm.

"Before we begin, I just want to say thanks. For the books, the help painting—everything. I know you don't think me fostering Kevin is the greatest idea in the world, but I'm going to make it work."

Her brown eyes shone with sincerity, and the last of his walls tumbled. "I know you will." He had no doubt she'd move heaven and earth to do the right thing, and as entrenched as his cynicism was, it couldn't stand against optimism like that. "Now let's get to work." Painting he could handle; this level of emotion was more than he'd signed up for.

Thankfully, despite her lack of experience, Dani had all the right equipment, and then some. She must have bought out half of Paradise's small hardware store. In no time they had a steady rhythm going, covering the stark white walls of what had been her office with a masculine blue. At least, Dani seemed to have a rhythm; he, on the other hand, kept getting distracted by the patch of skin that would peek out under the hem of her T-shirt every time she stretched onto her toes to push the paint roller to the top of the wall. And twice he'd dripped paint on himself when she'd bent over to pour more paint in the tray. After an hour of this torture he was hot and frustrated. The only consolation was that he was pretty sure he'd caught her checking him out, too.

"Can you give me a hand with this?" Dani asked, her back to him. "I can't get the lid off of this paint can to save my life."

He crossed to where she crouched, trying to keep his mind on the here and now. But damn if she didn't look gorgeous, even with paint smeared on her cheek and a look of frustration on her face. Dropping onto his knees beside her, he reached for the screwdriver in her hand. Her skin was warm and soft, like living silk. Without realizing what he was doing, he brushed his thumb across her palm, the caress drawing a startled breath from her.

Her eyes were wide, pupils dilated. He waited for her to pull her hand from his, to say or do something to end the moment. Instead, she leaned in. Just a fraction of an inch at first, as if she was testing the waters. Breath held, he waited, somehow knowing that she needed to be the one to come to him. His heart thudded in his chest, so loudly he thought surely she'd hear it. Then the pounding intensified, and it occurred to him that something other than his racing heart might be at play here.

Startled, she jerked back. "The door. My sister. Crap."

Pulse jumping, Dani stood and hurried to the door.

"Hey, Dani, you in there? What's going on?" her sister shouted from the other side of the door, pounding once again.

Crap, how long had Mollie been out there? How could she have let herself get so distracted? *Distracted* wasn't even the right word—she'd been completely oblivious to the outside world, as if she'd fallen under a spell. But she wasn't some fairy-tale princess, and she definitely wasn't looking to be swept off her feet. Maybe the paint fumes had been getting to her, making her feel off-kilter and dizzy. That had to be it. She'd open some windows, and turn on a fan or something before finishing up.

Running the last few steps to the door, she unlocked it and let her sister in.

"About time! I was getting ready to call the cops or something. What's going on?"

Dani shut the door and shrugged. "Nothing, I guess I just didn't hear you. I must have been in the zone, you know, painting."

Mollie looked over Dani's shoulder, and smirked. "Uh-huh. I can see how that might be very distracting. Painting, I mean."

Cheeks heating, she turned and found Tyler standing behind her. "Hi, you must be Dani's sister, Mollie. I'm Tyler—nice to meet you."

"Nice to meet you, too. Although I think we've actually met before. You have that cute little toy store, right? I've been in a few times to pick up things for my son. We got him that push-along fire truck last week, the one that has all the alphabet letters. He loves it."

"I remember! Your husband bought some model trains as well, right?"

Mollie smiled. "Yup, that's him. He's not happy if he's not building something with his hands. So I guess both my guys ended up happy that day."

"Glad to hear it."

Dani cleared her throat. "If you guys are done catching up, we do still have a room to put together."

Mollie rolled her eyes. "I was just making conversation with your...friend?" The implication that he might be more than that hung in the air.

"Helper. He's here to help with the room. And he

brought over some parenting books." Nothing romantic about that, at least.

"Really?" Mollie's eyes widened with curiosity.

"Yes, really." She had a feeling her sister would be peppering her with questions later, but for now, she needed to get things back on track. "Do you want to paint, or work on putting together the bedroom furniture I bought?"

Mollie eyed the paint smears on Tyler and Dani. "You two seem to have the paint thing in hand. I'll take furniture assembly." She looked around the living room and frowned. "That is, if I can find a flat surface to sit and work."

"My bedroom's still mostly clear. You can work in there if you want. And if you need any tools, they are under the kitchen sink."

"Perfect. I'm on it." She started for one of the bigger boxes, but Tyler grabbed it first.

"Just show me where you want it."

Mollie grinned up at him. "Thanks. This way."

Dani watched him restlessly, fighting the urge to run ahead of them and block the door. Having him in her bedroom, even if she wasn't there, felt too personal. At least she'd made the bed this morning. Of course, just thinking about her bed, and Tyler, had her imagining things that she had no business imagining. That she was even capable of fantasizing was pretty amazing, though, given her lack of libido for the past year. A step toward healing, but why did it have to happen *now*? Her world was already about to be turned upside down and inside out.

The best she could do was acknowledge the feelings, and set them aside to deal with later. Much later.

Determined to do just that, she turned her pent-up energy toward more productive matters. Namely, opening that stubborn paint can. Shoving the screwdriver under the edge of the lid with one hand, she pushed, and heard a pop. Yes! She dug a finger under the lifted lid and pulled, but it was still stuck. Wedging another finger in, she pulled again, hard, channeling her frustration into this one thing, telling herself if she could just get the damn lid off, everything would be okay.

Another pull, and the lid, and her fingernail, gave way. She swore viciously, and grabbed at her injured finger.

"Everything okay in here?" Tyler stood in the doorway, concern on his face. "I heard you yell from across the house."

"Yes. It's nothing." She tried to smile, but failed miserably.

"It didn't sound like nothing." His gaze took in the open can, the paint spatters and then her, as she cradled her injured finger in her other hand. "Did you hurt yourself?"

"I just broke a nail. Nothing serious." But damn it, it hurt.

"You're bleeding," he argued. "Do you have a first-aid kid somewhere?"

"In the hall closet. But I can handle it, really."

"I'm sure you can. But you don't have to." He disappeared, returning a minute later with the small kit she kept on hand for emergencies. "Let me take a look."

Giving up, she held out her finger, torn nail and all. "Like I said, it's nothing."

"Hush." He used an antiseptic wipe from the kit to clean away the small amount of blood, then deftly applied antibiotic ointment and a bandage. His touch should have been comforting rather than arousing, but the tension she felt in his presence lingered, like the scent of ozone after a storm.

"There, all better."

"Thanks." She swallowed, hesitated, not sure what else to say. "I could have done it myself, but thanks. For the help I mean. And the books. And—"

He put a finger to her lips, shushing her again. "Has anyone ever told you that you talk too much?"

His skin was warm against her lips, short-circuiting any ability to form words. She managed to shake her head, and he laughed, a soft chuckle.

"Dani Post, I don't think I believe you." Some part of her registered that she should protest, but before she could say anything he'd replaced his finger with his lips, and with his kiss she found she was, for once, absolutely speechless.

Tyler hadn't planned to kiss her. Fantasized about it, yes. But now that he had, it was blowing his fantasies out of the water. Her lips were soft and sweet, a tantalizing contrast to her sometimes sharp wit. She tasted like strawberries and honey, like everything good, and she felt even better.

Her mouth parted under his, and he took the kiss deeper, wrapping one arm around her as she buried her hands in his hair, holding him against her. Off balance, either from the angle or the sudden punch of adrenaline, he moved forward, searching for something solid. A few stumbling steps and he found purchase against the wall, freeing his other hand up to explore the delicate skin at the nape of her neck before tracing the shell of one ear. She moaned and arched back, giving him better access. Taking advantage, he trailed a line of kisses along her jaw, pressing closer when she moaned, his arm squeezed between her waist and the wall they leaned on.

Suddenly, she stiffened, her hands moving to his chest, pushing him away.

He eased back, as far as he could go with his arm still trapped behind her. "Hey, are you okay? I guess we got a little carried away there, huh?"

Her breathing rasped loudly in the quiet room, and her eyes darted from him to the door and back. Another shove, and he nearly fell. Pulling his arm free, he gave her some space, sensing there was more here than mild regret over a stolen kiss.

"Are you okay? Dani, talk to me." He'd hoped the irony of him begging her to talk just minutes after shutting her up with a kiss would have triggered a smart comeback, but she only shook her head once, then ran from the room. A minute later he heard the back door slam.

"What the hell just happened?" Mollie stuck her head in the door, concern on her face. "I was in the living room grabbing another box and Dani blew past me and ran out the back door like the house was on fire." She crossed her arms and glared at him. "What did you do?"

He threw his hands up in frustration. "I wish I knew! One minute we were kissing, and the next she was staring at me as if she'd never seen me before. It was crazy."

"Wait, you were kissing?"

Oops. Probably shouldn't have mentioned that part,

not without Dani's okay. "Yes, but don't say anything, okay? It was kind of…spontaneous. I'm not sure she wants it to be public knowledge."

Mollie huffed. "I'm her sister, not the public. But I won't mention it." She narrowed her eyes in thought. "You're sure she wanted the kiss, right?"

"Yes!" She'd been just as into it as he was, he was positive. "She was fine, and then all of a sudden she wasn't. It was like a switch flipped or something, almost like a panic attack." A memory surfaced. "It was a lot like when an army buddy of mine with PTSD had flashbacks. That same frightened, confused look coming out of nowhere. Little things could trigger him, things other people didn't even notice."

"Weird." Mollie chewed her lip in thought. "I have noticed that she's been a bit more on edge, a little more careful about things since she moved back. Like the door being locked this morning—she never used to lock her door during the day. And my dad says she never works late at the office. She'll stop in the middle of whatever she's working on and take it with her, just so she can be home by dark. Little things that, honestly I'd kind of blown off as just habits she picked up working in a big city. But with this, and how jumpy she's been, I'm wondering…"

"You're wondering if there's more going on with her." The thought that Dani might be fighting her own demons, on top of what she was taking on with Kevin, was sobering.

"I should go talk to her, find out what's going on." He headed for the back door.

"Let me," Mollie said. "I'm her sister. I should talk to her."

"You're not even supposed to know we kissed, so how are you going to ask her about this? Let me try. If nothing else, I want to apologize for whatever I did to freak her out. I owe her that."

Biting her lip, Mollie considered, then slowly nodded. "Fine, but you better not make things worse. Or I'll have to hurt you."

Tyler bit back a grin at the diminutive woman's threat. He probably had a hundred pounds on her, but he had no doubt she was serious. "I promise. If she doesn't want to talk about it, I'll just apologize and leave. I'm not going to force her to do anything." Hopefully his meaning was clear. He would never force himself upon a woman, physically or emotionally.

"Good. You'll probably find her on the dock, down by the pond. There's a path that runs behind the building that will take you there. It's small, and no one ever really uses it, but she likes to sit there sometimes."

"Thanks."

He found the path easily enough—it was a narrow, paved walkway that took him past a maintenance building of some sort and then angled down toward a small retention pond. On the far side he made out a figure sitting on a floating dock, her back to him. Bingo.

Not wanting to spook her, he called out before stepping onto the dock. "Hey, room for two out there?"

She turned, and he saw the unmistakable tracks of tears on her face. Regret hit him like a punch to the gut. He'd done this. Never mind that he hadn't meant to, he'd scared her, made her cry. "Crap, Dani, I'm sorry."

"Don't be." She sniffed, and wiped at her face. "It's not your fault. You didn't do anything wrong. Really."

A bit of his guilt eased at her reassurance. "Okay

if I sit with you for a bit?" No way was he taking one step into her space without her express permission.

She shrugged, and then when he didn't move, nodded briefly. "If you want. I'm surprised you'd want to. I figured you'd just go home after I ran out like that."

He sat down on the sun-warmed boards: close enough to talk easily but far enough away to give her a bit of space. "Nah, I don't scare that easily. Besides, you seemed like you might need someone to talk to, once you had a chance to catch your breath." When she didn't say anything, he continued. "I have a friend, good guy, who did a few tours in Iraq. When he came back, he'd have what he called episodes. Something would set him off, maybe a sound on TV, maybe a smell, maybe just someone getting a little too close, and his brain would kind of short-circuit, and for a minute he'd be right back in the war zone. Really messed with his head, not knowing when it might happen. He started isolating himself, spending more time at home."

She looked up, and he noticed her breathing was steadier, and her eyes had lost that frightened-animal look they'd had earlier. "What happened to him?"

"He got help. Therapy, and some medication. And he talked about it, a lot. Said that every time he told someone about what he'd been through, it helped to make it a part of his past, rather than his present. Not to mention, once his friends knew, they could try to avoid doing stuff to set him off, and they understood what was happening if he did have an episode."

"That makes sense, I guess." She swung her feet, her toes making ripples in the water. "It's hard though— to talk, I mean."

He laughed. "Dani, you haven't ever struck me as someone at a loss for words. You've certainly thrown a few at me when the mood suited you."

She smiled, and his heart settled. It seemed he couldn't quite breathe right when she was upset. Which made what he was about to ask her all the harder. It was going to upset her, and that would upset him. But if he wanted to help her, there was no way around it. "So, can you tell me about it? Can you tell me who hurt you?"

Chapter Six

Dani swallowed hard. Could she tell him? So far the only person she'd opened up to had been her therapist, and she'd only started that out of desperation. She'd started worrying she was crazy and had figured if anyone would know for sure, it was a psychologist. Talking about it, even with a professional, was draining and painful, but she'd heard some truth in what Tyler said. As hard as it was, talking about it *had* helped. Maybe it was time to open up outside of the shrink's office, if only so they'd know what was going on if she freaked out again. She'd been putting off telling her family. Their concern would overwhelm her, and she wasn't ready for that. But Tyler, he wouldn't smother her. And he seemed to have at least a modest grasp of PTSD and what it meant.

Taking a deep breath, she just said it. "When I was

working in Jacksonville, one of the junior partners tried to rape me. I got away, but it messed with my head, and I've been seeing a therapist for the past year, trying to work through it all." She watched him out of the corner of her eye, too nervous to face him, but needing to see his reaction.

A muscle along Tyler's jaw twitched, but his voice was calm when he spoke. "I'm so sorry."

That simple apology, from a man who owed her none, triggered something inside her that all her soul-searching hadn't been able to. Tears began to flow, silent at first, and then before she knew it she was sobbing, hugging her knees to her chest as she cried the way she hadn't let herself before.

Tyler reached out and put a cool hand on hers, and just sat, quietly, letting her cry. He didn't try to stop her, or tell her everything was okay. He just sat and waited, holding her hand. And somehow that helped. After a few minutes the sobs eased, and her breathing slowed as the emotions she'd been holding back for so long found a release. Finally, with no tears left, she uncurled and looked over at him. "Sorry. I don't normally do that."

"I figured as much. Sometimes it's the only thing to do, though. If you hold all the emotion in, it just builds up. Gotta let it out so it doesn't take over."

She nodded, feeling incredibly self-conscious all of a sudden. Here she was, with red eyes and a stuffy nose, and he was spouting advice as if this kind of thing happened to him all the time. Of course, he had two daughters; maybe he'd had practice with crying females. "Did your daughters teach you that?"

He shook his head, and looked out toward the horizon. "No, losing my wife did."

"Oh." Somehow she'd forgotten he had his own trauma, his own pain. "You really loved her, didn't you?"

"I did. We met at college orientation, and got married the day after graduation. She had the twins nine months later. I thought life was perfect, and then everything fell apart. I tried to be strong, for the girls, for myself, but it started to kill me, all that pent-up emotion. It wasn't until I really let myself grieve, that I was able to move on and really be there for my girls."

She nodded. It made sense, and explained why he was able to handle her grief. He'd had plenty of his own to deal with. Maybe that was why he was easier to talk to than her family. They had such happy lives; she hated to taint any of it with her own ugly story.

As if sensing her thoughts, he stretched out, leaning back on his arms, getting comfortable, before he asked, almost casually, "So, want to tell me the whole story? It might help, and I'm a good listener."

"That you are." Mimicking his pose, she tried to relax as she struggled to find a place to start. "When I finished law school, I was recruited by a few firms, mostly smaller places. But one guy in particular showed an interest, from a big, fairly prestigious practice in Jacksonville. He said I showed promise, that I'd have a fast track to the top if I signed with his firm. He bought me expensive dinners and basically told me everything I wanted to hear." She paused, remembering how easily he'd reeled her in. "I was an idiot, to think that he meant any of it."

"No, you weren't. Maybe a bit naive, but he's the one to blame here, not you."

"Maybe," she conceded. "Anyway, when I took the job, he continued to pay a lot of attention to me. At first, I was flattered. I thought he was impressed by my talent, my work ethic. But then it got a bit weird, more like flirting. And I knew he was married." She paused, letting the beauty of the surroundings ease some of the tension in her body. "I talked to a few co-workers and found out he had a reputation, to say the least. Touching female employees, that kind of thing. I started avoiding him, making excuses so I wouldn't have to be alone with him. It worked, mostly, and I guess I let down my guard. One night, I stayed late to try to finish up some research. I was the only person left on my floor, and he found me." The words came slower now, as if the weight of the memory made them harder to say. "I was at my desk. He came in, and closed the door. I got up, thinking if I could just leave, it would be okay. But before I could take two steps, he was there. He told me I'd been playing hard to get, that it had worked. That I was going to get his undivided attention now, just like I wanted." Her voice cracked, and she swallowed to clear the lump from her throat.

"Dani, if this is too hard—"

"No, I want to finish." She needed to finish, to say it out loud. "He pressed me against the wall, and started pulling up my skirt. I knew then he was going to rape me, and there was no one around to stop him. I almost gave up, right then. But then I remembered my key chain." She smiled. "My dad gave it to me, on my sixteenth birthday. It has a pocketknife on it, engraved with my name. I kept it on my desk. The small blade made a perfect letter opener. Somehow, I managed to reach it. I held it to his throat, and I told him that if he didn't get off of me, I'd kill him."

Listening to Dani tell her story, he had no doubt that she meant it. She would have killed to protect herself, and he respected the hell out of her for her strength. "You're incredibly brave. I take it he left then?"

She grimaced. "Yeah, he left. Ran out, calling me a crazy bitch, saying he'd get me fired."

"What? Did he really say that?"

"He did. And he would have done it if I'd given him the chance. Instead, I quit."

Tyler's head started to hurt. "Why? He was the one that was in the wrong, not you. He attacked you, for God's sake—he should be in jail."

"Yeah, well, in a perfect world, maybe. In reality, I'd already reported him for sexual harassment and been told to stop making trouble. He was a partner. He had value to the company. I was nobody. It was his word against mine and mine didn't count. So I wrote out a resignation letter, packed my stuff and left. I moved home the next day."

"What about the police?"

A flicker of doubt whipped across her face, and then was gone. She drew her legs back up to her body and rested her chin on her knees. "I didn't report it. It would have been the same situation, his word against mine. There was no proof. Since he hadn't actually raped me, no physical evidence."

"Thank God!"

"Yeah, well, like I said, the reality is that means there was no evidence. I'd already been humiliated in front of my boss for daring to say anything. I wasn't up for another round of that with the police. I just wanted to get home."

"You wanted to be safe. That's natural. That you managed to get away from him at all is nothing short of amazing. You're a tough lady, Dani Post."

"My shrink says the same thing. But I don't feel tough. I feel like I let myself down. That I should have stayed and reported him, even if it didn't amount to anything. I hate the thought that he could do this to someone else."

"You can't take on that burden. Not when you are still healing yourself. Besides, after what you did, maybe he'll think twice about cornering unsuspecting women. I think having a knife held to your throat would certainly inspire a person to reexamine their life choices."

"Maybe." She turned and looked at him, her features both delicate and determined. "But I'm not going to feel strong, or brave, when I end up running off like a scared rabbit over a little kiss."

"Hey, that wasn't just a little kiss. That was a very intense, passionate kiss. Possibly the best kiss I've ever had."

She laughed, and he felt the need to make sure she continued to have laughter in her life. She deserved that. And more.

"Fine, it was a mind-blowing kiss. But the point is, I freaked out. How can I move on, and live my life, when I can't stand to be touched?"

He thought, and realized she was missing an important clue. "But you didn't panic from being touched or from the kiss. You didn't get scared until you were against the wall. Which makes sense. You associated being pinned to the wall with your attack. That's what caused the flashback."

"Maybe." She sounded unsure, but there was an element of hope in her voice, too.

"There's a way to test that theory out, you know. When you're up for it."

"Let me guess—you think we should kiss again?"

"Only if you want to." He was serious about that. He didn't want to do anything more to scare her off.

"I might freak out again," she warned. "I could shove you in the lake or something if I panic."

"I know how to swim." He took her hand again, rubbing the soft skin with his thumb. "I'm not afraid of you, Dani, or what you're going through. It's not about me. It's about what you want, and what works for you."

She shivered, whether at his touch or his words, he didn't know. "I'm scared."

"Then we won't do it. We don't have to do anything that you don't want to do."

"I didn't say I don't want to, I said I'm scared. But I'm also tired of letting my fears control my life."

He stilled, needing to know he was reading her right. "What are you saying?"

"I'm saying I want you to kiss me."

Dani couldn't believe it was her voice saying those words, asking Tyler to kiss her. But she'd come so close, and didn't want her panic attack to be what she remembered about today. If he was right, if it had been the situation, not the kiss, that had set her off, she needed to know that. And, more than any of that, she *wanted* to kiss him again.

At first, Tyler didn't move, and she wondered if he was going to turn her down. A sob story about being nearly raped was hardly a turn-on. Maybe, despite his kind words, he didn't want to get involved in the mess that was her life.

But then he shifted closer, his hand still tracing intimate patterns on her palm. Eyes open this time, she watched him, forcing her mind to recognize that this was Tyler, the single dad to twins, the man who ran a toy shop for a living. He was safe.

Only when their lips touched did she finally close her eyes, letting herself just enjoy the moment. And kissing Tyler Jackson was certainly enjoyable. He let her set the pace, holding back as she explored his mouth, the taste of his lips, the feel of his teeth against her tongue. Their joined hands were the only other point of contact, and even there he had loosened his grip, gently stroking rather than holding her hand. She had total freedom; he gave that to her, and she ran with it.

Deepening the kiss, she trailed her free hand across his chest, noting the hard muscle underneath, and then up to tangle in his hair. When she nipped at his lip he moaned, but didn't move. Emboldened, she shifted her legs toward him, coming up on her knees, one on each side of him, straddling him. Still he held still, giving her total control. She appreciated that, but fear wasn't what was coursing through her body right now. Lust was. Good, old-fashioned lust, the kind that melted your insides and put every nerve ending on sensory overload. And that kind of need couldn't be satisfied by half measures.

"Touch me," she whispered against his mouth before moving to explore the stubbled line of his jaw.

A groan was his response, and then his hands were on her, running up and down her sides before latching onto her butt to pull her firmly against him. "Is that okay?" he asked, his voice thick with desire.

"Mmmmmm," she moaned into his neck, wiggling herself even closer to him as he kissed his way down her neck. When he traced her collarbone with his tongue, she thought she might die from pleasure. Then he moved one hand to her breast, and she was sure she already had. Nothing on earth could feel this good.

"Dani?"

"What? Oh, don't stop." She arched into his hand, only to have him move it back to her side and smooth down her shirt.

"Trust me, I don't want to, but we're in full view of the public here."

It took a minute for his words to register, but when they did, she scrambled out of his lap in less than a heartbeat. "Oh, my God, we just... Where anyone could see us!"

"I believe the term is *making out*, and yes, anyone could see us, although I don't think anyone did."

She glanced around, certain one of her busybody neighbors would be watching, but as far as she could tell, he was right. They were alone, for now. "If you hadn't stopped things..." She trailed off, her face heating at the thought.

"We might have really put on a show, yeah, I know. I don't think either of us expected things to heat up quite that quickly."

She shook her head, still off-kilter from the hormones swirling through her body. "It's never been like that before. Maybe just because it's been so long…"

"Maybe, but I haven't been a complete monk, and that about knocked me off my feet, too. I don't think we need to analyze why, but we probably should get back to your apartment before your sister sends out a search party."

"I totally forgot about Mollie. Oops." A nervous giggle bubbled up. "I begged and begged her to help me today, and then when she shows up I vanish."

"I think she'll forgive you. But Dani, you should think about telling her what happened. She's worried about you."

"Mollie? Why?"

He stood, giving her his hand to help her up. "You've kept it together really well, but she knows you, and she's noticed things. Little things, but still. She's concerned."

That wasn't something she'd considered. She'd been avoiding telling her family to spare them, but maybe that was impossible to do. Still, she wasn't quite ready for that level of emotional fallout. "I'll think about it. Not now, but I'll think about it."

"Good enough." Keeping her hand in his, he started back toward the path.

Looking down at their joined hands, she pulled him to a stop. "Listen, Tyler, about what just happened… Can we keep that between us, for now?"

"Um…about that." He shrugged innocently. "I may have let it slip to Mollie, before I came out here, that we'd kissed."

"What? Why?"

"I didn't mean to, but I was worried about you, and Mollie was acting like I might have done something to hurt you, so I told her the truth, that we'd kissed."

"And how did she react to that bit of information?"

"She didn't, really. She was more focused on why you ran out than on your love life. She did say that you hadn't dated much recently."

The understatement of the year. "Well, for now, I think maybe it needs to stay that way." Tyler frowned. "It's not that I'm not attracted to you. Obviously I am."

"Is it because of the attack? Do you need to slow things down? Because we can do that—I meant what I said. I don't want to push you."

"No. Yes. Maybe."

He arched an eyebrow at her conflicting answer.

"I don't know. I do know that I'm dealing with a lot of crazy stuff right now. The attack is part of it, yes. Despite how…well things went just now, I'm not sure I'm ready to be in a relationship. And on top of that, even if I was, I've got Kevin to think about. He has to be my main priority right now. Can you understand that?" She looked up at him, silently begging him to understand.

He shoved a hand through his hair, his jaw clenched. Finally, he nodded. "Yeah, I can understand that. But for the record, I think you're capable of more than you give yourself credit for. I think we might be really good together. But if you need time to sort things out, I can wait."

"Thanks." She gave his hand a quick squeeze before dropping it. Instantly, she missed the sense of connection. "So are we friends?"

"Friends." He sighed. "Let me guess, that means I still have to help you paint, but I don't get to kiss you."

"Pretty much, yeah."

"Then I guess we'd better get back to work."

Chapter Seven

Dani stood looking through the shop window, trying to get up the courage to walk in. She had no real reason for the butterflies somersaulting in her stomach; she and Tyler were friends. That was all. After their little kiss they'd gone back to the apartment and painted as if nothing had happened. At least, outwardly that was the case. Inside she'd been a tangle of questions. Should she have kissed him? Should she have told him about what happened in Jacksonville? Would he keep her secret? But despite her doubts, she didn't regret what had happened. Part of her wished she'd felt ready to try for more, to continue seeing him in that way. The other part of her was scared just to walk into his shop.

But that was ridiculous. Besides, she had things to buy and didn't have time to waste standing around second-guessing herself. Inhaling, she straightened her shoulders and pulled open the door. A bell tinkled above her, announcing her presence. Behind the counter was Tyler, and at the sound he looked up and smiled.

"Hi, it's nice to see you."

Self-consciously she smoothed a hand over her dress. "You, too. But I'm here to shop today. I want to pick up a few things for Kevin, for when he moves in this weekend."

Tyler's smile wavered just a bit. "Right, of course. What were you thinking?"

She shrugged. "Honestly, I'm not sure. I know he likes baseball, and maybe it's a terrible idea, but I was thinking I could get him the bat he wanted. But I don't want him to think I'm rewarding him for bad behavior, you know?"

Tyler shook his head. "I think that buying him the thing he tried to steal might send the wrong message. What about some building toys? Those are pretty popular with kids his age, and help build spatial awareness and problem-solving skills." He grinned. "Plus, they're fun."

"Thanks, that sounds great. Point me to them."

Tyler led her to an aisle crowded with sets of plastic bricks, each box promising a different craft or structure could be made. "Umm…any idea which ones would be good? Some of these look pretty complex."

"The suggested age ranges are on the boxes, in the corner there. Beyond that, it's just what looks fun. This one is pretty popular right now." He held up a box depicting a spaceship from a popular movie series.

"Sold." She shook her head, scanning the aisle for another set. "Just when I'm starting to think I can really do this, I realize I'm totally clueless. How am I going to handle parenting full-time when I can't even figure out what toys to buy him?"

"You're being too hard on yourself. Overthinking things. It's just a toy. Either he'll like it, or he won't. You don't have to be perfect, you know."

"Don't I?" It felt that way.

"No such thing as a perfect parent. Ask my kids sometime. I'm sure they can tell you a half-dozen things I've done wrong just in the past week."

As if on cue, the children in question stepped out from around the corner. "He's right. He makes mistakes all the time."

"Lots of them," the other twin chimed in.

Tyler rolled his eyes. "Thanks a lot, guys."

"Hey, they are just agreeing with you." Dani smiled at the cuties, motioning them closer. "So tell me, what does your daddy do that's so terrible?"

The one in pink, who seemed to be the bolder of the two, tapped a finger on her forehead as if thinking. "Well, the big thing right now is that he keeps forgetting to get us a kitten."

"Oh, really?"

"Uh-huh!" the one in yellow agreed. "He promised and promised to get us a kitty, but he never does."

Dani turned back to Tyler, desperately trying not to laugh. "Is this true, sir?"

"Yes, okay, I'm guilty as charged. But in my defense, I've been pretty busy. And the animal shelter's hours aren't very convenient." He sighed. "But they're right, I did promise. Like I said, no one's perfect."

"It seems not." She turned back to the girls. "How

about I see if I can help your dad out on this one. Would that be okay?"

Two sets of identical blue eyes shined back at her. "Yes!"

"Yes, please."

"Oops, I mean yes please," Adelaide corrected.

Dani did laugh this time. She couldn't help it. "I'll see what I can do."

"All right, that's enough browbeating for one day. You two need to go finish your homework, and then I'll come and check it, okay?"

"Okay," they said in unison, running off down the aisle.

"Sorry about that," he said.

"Nothing to be sorry about. They're adorable. Which one was in the pink?"

"The instigator you mean? That's Adelaide. She's the feisty one. Amy is a lot quieter, but don't let that fool you—she's just as likely to get into trouble."

"Just less likely to get caught," Dani mused.

"Exactly."

"Sounds like my sister and me. I was the quieter, more well-behaved one. At least when my parents were looking."

"And yet somehow I bet you got into plenty of trouble yourself."

"I did." Just standing here, looking at Tyler, bantering with him, felt like it could lead to trouble. Time to steer the conversation back to safer ground. "Speaking of which, I meant what I said about helping out with the kitten situation. But only if you're serious about getting them one."

"I am." He leaned against the shelf behind him,

casual but wary. "Do you have some kind of connection to the kitten black market I should be aware of?"

She grinned. "Actually, I do. One of my friends is a veterinarian. She and her father own Paradise Animal Clinic. They've almost always got a batch of foster animals that need homes."

"Huh, I hadn't even thought to check there. Well, I would appreciate it, if you can work something out. But don't I remember you saying you had your hands full right now?"

She flushed at his obvious reference to her reasons for not pursing a relationship. "I'm busy, yes, but this really isn't any trouble. I can stop by the clinic tomorrow on my lunch hour. It won't take but a minute." Besides, it wasn't the time that was her biggest concern when it came to dating Tyler. It was the emotional maelstrom that threatened to overwhelm her every time they touched. Kissing Tyler had been like grabbing onto a lightning bolt, and she couldn't afford to get burned.

He shouldn't have pushed her. As soon as he'd made the remark about her being too busy to help, he'd realized it was a mistake. She'd smiled, and her response had been friendly enough, but she'd left almost immediately. He didn't even know why he'd said it; it wasn't like he expected her to say, "You're right, Tyler. If I have the time and energy to ask about an orphan kitten, I definitely have room in my life for a relationship with you!" No, the chances of that happening were about the same as the chances of his daughters taking a liking to brussels sprouts. But he just hadn't been able to keep his bruised ego from taking control of his big mouth.

Nothing to do about it now. Bringing it back up would just make things more awkward. Better to pretend it didn't happen and focus on the present. Which today meant another mentoring visit with Kevin. His foster parents were going to drop him off at the shop after school, and he had arranged for a babysitter to watch the girls. He'd like them to make friends, but for now Kevin needed some one-on-one time.

The jingle of the bell over the front door let him know his young friend had arrived. "Hey, Mr. Tyler! What are we doing today?"

Tyler waved out the window at the Cunninghams, then faced the boy, hands on his hips. "Well, that depends. We have two choices, and you get to decide which we do. What do you say we discuss it over a snack?"

"Sounds good, I'm starving."

Tyler grinned. From what he remembered of his own childhood, growing boys were in a perpetual state of near starvation. "Well, come on then, we can't have you wasting away." He motioned Kevin into the back room, where he had brownies, several kinds of fruit and milk waiting. "Think this will tide you over?"

"Oh, man, yeah!" He sat at the table and took a swig of milk. "Can I have two brownies?"

"Let's start with one brownie and a piece of fruit. If you're still hungry after that, you can have another one."

"Okay," he agreed, his mouth already full.

Tyler sat across from him and took one for himself. "Wow, these are good."

"You didn't make them?"

"Me? No." Tyler shook his head. "I bought these at the Sandcastle Bakery. I can cook enough to get by, but this is way beyond my abilities."

"Mrs. Cunningham used to bake me things all the time, but she's been more tired lately. Not that I care," he added hastily. "I don't need cookies and stuff all the time. But..."

"But you're worried about her."

Thin shoulders shrugged. "I guess. I mean, I'm not a sissy about it or anything. But she's old, and when I move in with Dani, who's going to help her and Mr. C.?"

Tyler heart twisted. He'd expected Kevin to be worried about himself, and the transition. Instead, the boy was concerned about his foster parents. Once again he was reminded that kids, even kids that got into trouble, were innocent and selfless in a way most adults could only hope to emulate. "Well, they are going to move into a senior living center. Do you know what that is?"

Kevin reached for a banana and shook his head.

"Well, it's a special place for older people who might need extra help. They have nurses and other people there that will check up on the Cunninghams every day, to make sure they are doing okay. And they have a restaurant there, so if they don't feel up to cooking they can just go downstairs and have a healthy meal whenever they want. And they even have game nights, and activities for them to join."

Relief washed over the little boy's face. "So they are going to be okay?"

"Absolutely. And I know they wouldn't want you

worrying about them. What they want is for you to work hard in school, and to stay out of trouble."

"Can I go visit?"

"Of course. I'm sure Dani would be happy to take you to see them, or I can take you, too, if you want." He made a mental note to let the Cunninghams and Dani know about the child's concerns. Together they could help him, but only if they were all on the same page.

"Cool." Relieved of his worry, he went back to eating, not coming back up for air until he'd finished his fruit, two brownies and a full glass of milk. Wiping his face with his sleeve, he tilted his head and asked, "So, what are these options you said I had?"

Tyler straightened. He was pretty sure he knew what the boy would choose, but there was a chance his offer would be seen as an insult to the tentative friendship they'd forged. But if his gut was right, it was worth the risk. "Well, we could go down to the park and hang out, or..."

"Or what?"

"Or we could stay here, and I could give you a job."

"A job?" His eyes narrowed. "You mean like some kind of servant or something?"

"No, like an employee."

"Wait, you'd pay me?"

"Sort of." Kevin frowned "Wait, hear me out. I was thinking you could work toward earning a new baseball bat of your choice."

Kevin stared, eyes wide. "Wait, you'd give me the bat that I stole from you? Are you serious?"

"Not give. You'd earn it. It's okay to want things, Kevin, but it's important to go about getting them in the right way. Earning it will take more time and effort than stealing, but every time you use it you can be proud of how you got it."

"Did Dani tell you to do this?"

"No. She wanted to buy you one." Oops. Probably shouldn't have let that bit of information out.

He nodded, sandy brown hair falling over his eyes. "Yeah, that sounds like her. But I'd rather earn it."

"Really?" Now that he wouldn't have expected.

"Uh-huh. That way it will be really mine, you know? Lots of times grown-ups will give you stuff to use, but you don't always get to keep it. But if I earn it, then it's mine forever, right?"

Tyler nodded, his throat tight. He hadn't considered that. Most foster kids didn't get to accumulate stuff; they moved too often. Obviously Kevin was no exception. "Forever."

"Then tell me what to do, boss. I'm ready to work."

Dani had a dilemma. An incredibly adorable, furry dilemma, purring in her lap.

"So, did you make up your mind yet?" Cassie asked from across the room, where she was giving an elderly Chihuahua a physical exam.

"No. They're both too cute. I can't pick between them." It had taken her several days to find the time to make it over to Paradise Animal Clinic, but in a stroke of luck Cassie said she had not one, but two orphan kittens in need of adoption. Perfect. She'd pick the cutest, cuddliest one and take it right over to Tyler's shop for his girls.

By the time she realized her mistake, it was too late.

As it turns out, *all* kittens were cute and cuddly. Instantly, they'd both stolen her heart. One was grey and white with big green eyes, and the other was orange like Garfield. Both gave the word *adorable* new meaning. She watched as they tumbled and played, using her legs as a jungle gym, and sighed. "They seem to really be bonded to each other, aren't they?"

"Well, they are litter mates. They've been together since birth," Cassie answered without looking up, her attention focused on her patient. "But they'd adapt. Of course, it would be harder on the one left behind." She finished examining the petite pet's teeth, and glanced over. "Of course...you could always take both of them."

Dani shook her head. "No, I couldn't do that. Tyler said one kitten."

"One, two...it's not really any more work with kittens. Puppies, yes, but with kittens it can actually be easier. They play with each other and tire each other out. They can share a litter box and food bowl and everything."

"Really?" Hope blossomed. She really didn't want to separate them, and after all, there *were* two girls. When you thought about it, two kittens made sense. Right?

"Sure. And if he totally freaks, you can always bring one back." Cassie grinned. "But I doubt he'll be able to choose between them any more than you can."

"Wait, you knew this was going to happen, didn't you?"

She shrugged. "I had a good idea."

"Ugh. So not fair. Tyler's going to kill me." But even as she said it, she knew she wasn't leaving one of the kittens behind.

"I highly doubt that. Word is that he's pretty into you."

Dani tensed. "Where did you hear that?"

"I don't know, a few places. People have seen you and him together, with Kevin, and it seems the general consensus is that the man has the hots for you."

Dani rolled her eyes. "If gossip was a sport, Paradise could field its own team."

"So are you saying it isn't true?"

Lying to her friend wasn't an option, but she also didn't want to feed the rumor mill. "What I'm saying is that we're friends, and only friends. I'm going to have too much going on once Kevin moves in to add any more drama in my life right now."

"In other words, he was interested, but you turned him down. Interesting." Cassie shook her head. "You know, there's no rule against dating just because you're a parent. Or foster parent. If I'd stuck with that attitude, I wouldn't have Alex. Or little Sophia." Cassie's eyes softened at the mention of her husband and their new baby.

"Your situation was a bit different. You'd been a single mom for years before you met him. It's not like you were dating right after having Emma. You took time to settle into the role, and that's all I'm asking for."

Her friend nodded reluctantly. "That's true, and I do understand what you're saying. I just know that sometimes love finds us when we least expect it. Keep an open mind, okay?"

"Fine." There was no point in arguing with Cassie once she had something in her head. "But right now, I'm focusing on Kevin."

"Then why are you here, picking out kittens?"

"Because... Because it was something a friend

would do for another friend. And that's what Tyler and I are—friends. Just friends."

"Right. Got it." Cassie winked. "But for the record, you blush when you say his name."

Fifteen minutes later, after threatening her friend to knock it off or find another home for the kittens, Dani walked into Tropical Toys with a borrowed cat carrier in one hand and a bag of cat supplies in the other. Tyler, at the front counter, spotted her right away and grinned knowingly. "I thought you were just going to ask about a kitten? But I guess it's just as well—the girls are going to be so excited."

"About that…"

"Wait, let me get them. They're going to want to hear everything." He turned away and called, "Amy! Addie! Come see what Miss Dani brought!"

Dani started to speak, then bit her tongue. She'd planned on having a few minutes to discuss the situation with Tyler first, but already the girls were running in, curiosity shining in their eyes. She'd just have to hope that Tyler was flexible.

"What's in the box?"

"What did you bring?"

"Can we see?"

"Me, first!"

"Whoa…settle down, you'll frighten them."

"Them?" Tyler cocked an eyebrow. "What do you mean *them*?"

Dani avoided meeting his gaze, instead turning her attention to the two girls. "I'll open the box, but you have to be gentle, okay?" When the girls nodded she undid the top of the carrier, revealing the two fur balls inside.

"Kittens!"

"Two kittens!"

"Two kittens?" Tyler rounded the counter to check for himself. By the time he got to the box, each of his daughters held a small kitten, looks of rapture upon their faces. "Um, Dani?"

"Well… Cassie said it was better to adopt them out together, because they can tire each other out that way. And they were so bonded to each other I couldn't bear to separate them." She stopped, knowing that wasn't an excuse. "But still, I should have checked with you first, I'm sorry. Cassie did say I could take one of them back, if you want."

"Right, like I could do that. Look at them."

Dani did look, and felt her heart actually melt into a gooey puddle at the sight. The girls were sitting on the floor, side by side, each snuggling one of the tiny kittens. From what she could tell from their conversation, they were already discussing suitable names. "I see your point. If it helps, I brought all the supplies they'll need for the first few weeks. A litter box, litter, food, bowls and collars."

"You didn't have to do all that. Our pets, our responsibility."

"Consider it a peace offering, restitution for springing an extra cat on you."

He looked again at the girls, giggling sweetly over their new pets, and sighed. "Honestly, it's probably for the best. If you'd brought only one, they would be fighting over who gets to hold it, who gets to feed it… You've probably saved me a ton of aggravation. So thanks, I guess."

"You're welcome, I guess." Relief washed over her. "So, where should I put all this stuff?"

"Let's set everything up in the back room for now." He took the bag of supplies from her, leading the way. "So, how are preparations for Kevin going?"

"Good. I had my final home visit yesterday and I finished the parenting course. His room is all ready, thanks to you and Mollie. All that's left is to pick him up on Saturday and move him in." She paused, a ribbon of tension tightening in her belly. "Why, did he say something about it to you? Is he upset about moving in with me?"

"Calm down, nothing like that. I was just curious. Although I do think he's got more on his mind than he's been letting on."

"What do you mean?"

"Well, he's worried about the Cunninghams. He feels a bit like he's abandoning them. He sees himself a bit as their caretaker, as much as they are his."

"Oh, no! I hadn't even thought of that."

"Me, either, but don't worry, I think I reassured him on that score. I explained that they'd be well taken care of at the assisted-living facility, and promised him he could visit, to check up on them."

"Of course he can. I'll be happy to take him, whenever he wants!"

"That's exactly what I told him. And I promised him I'd be willing to take him over there, too, if he'd like."

"Thanks. But I should have been the one to find this out. I'm going to be his foster parent and I had no idea he was worried about them. I thought he'd be nervous about the move, about living in a new place, but that he's so concerned about the Cunninghams…it never occurred to me."

Tyler put a hand on her arm. "Hey, don't go there. I didn't think of it, either. He just happened to tell me at our last mentoring session. I'm sure he'll talk to you about it as well, when you see him."

More guilt churned in her belly. "Ugh, I haven't seen him in over a week. That's got to be confusing to him—to have me saying I want to foster him while ignoring him in the meantime."

"He knows that you're busy doing everything you need to do to be approved as a foster parent. He doesn't blame you for that. And you shouldn't blame yourself. What you are doing takes a tremendous amount of time and effort, and it's to your credit that you are doing it at all."

"This from the guy who said it was a dumb idea for me to foster?" she teased.

"Hey, I can admit when I'm wrong." He took both of her hands in his, sending tingles of awareness through her body. "Talking to him about everything made me realize how lucky he is to have you. You'll make sure his emotional needs are met, not just his physical ones. You'll take him to visit the Cunninghams and will listen when he is worried, or scared, or just needs to talk. Another foster family might have more experience, but there is a good chance they wouldn't have time for all of that. You're just what he needs."

Dani stood, breathless at his words. Again, he'd said exactly what she needed to hear. Which was exactly what made this so hard. After a speech like that, all she wanted to do was step into his arms. It would be so easy. And yet she couldn't do it and keep her emotions in check. She had to keep her head about her right now. She'd worked too hard to reclaim her life; she was making too much progress to risk it all now on a whim.

Chapter Eight

Tyler looked around the spartan but clean room at the Cunninghams' and tried not to frown. Kevin had been living here for months but it looked almost like a hotel room, bare of the normal flotsam that kids tended to collect. No posters on the walls or favorite toys on display. There was a small dresser and matching nightstand, both dark and heavy and the kind of thing you'd expect to see in the bedroom of an older adult, and a bed neatly made with a plain green spread. The only personal item was a single framed photo of a lovely young woman. Kevin's mom, he'd guess. Compared to some foster situations it was more than adequate, but still, Tyler's heart hurt to compare it to his own girls' room, full of stuffed animals and scribbled pictures and life.

He couldn't let Kevin pick up on his feelings,

though. So he forced a smile, and set the suitcase he'd brought from home on the bed. "All right, buddy, let's get you packed."

He'd volunteered to help the boy pack up his things, thinking it might be a bit much for the Cunninghams to handle. Now, looking around, he realized he'd overestimated the task. Still, he was here now and by the looks of it they'd make quick work of the chore.

Kevin just shrugged, so Tyler went ahead and unzipped the suitcase, then headed for the dresser. "Okay if I just put everything in there together? I'll help you sort it out when we get to Dani's."

Another shrug. Not good.

Turning back around, Tyler took a seat on the narrow bed, next to where Kevin sat with hunched shoulders. "Everything okay, buddy?"

"I guess."

"You know, you can talk to me. Especially when you're feeling scared or confused. That's kind of the point of this whole mentor thing."

Kevin lower lip trembled, but he continued to sit, stone-faced, staring at the wall. How could he get through to him?

"Are you still worried about the Cunninghams? Because I told you, they're going to be fine. We can even help them move when the time comes, if you want."

A shake of the head. Okay, that wasn't it.

"Are you worried about living with Dani? That you won't like it there?"

He started to nod, then shook his head violently. This was going nowhere.

"Listen, Kevin, just talk to me, okay, fella? I can't read minds and playing twenty questions doesn't seem to be working. Give a guy a break, huh, and just tell me what's wrong. I can't help if I don't know."

"I'm not afraid I won't like it there. I'm sure I will. Dani's great. But what if she doesn't like living with me? She's not used to having a kid around. The Cunninghams, they've had tons of foster kids. Dani's never had any. What if I get there and she decides I'm too much trouble?"

That the boy's words mirrored Tyler's own early concerns didn't give him any pleasure. Thankfully he had a better appreciation of her tenacity and grit now than he'd had when she'd first told him of her plan. Kevin did, too, if he'd stop and think about it. "So what are you saying? You think Dani's a quitter?"

The boy's eyes widened. "No. Of course not."

"You think she's weak?"

He shook his head vehemently. "No."

"That's right, she's not. She's determined, and strong, and pretty stubborn, too, but don't tell her I said that. From everything I know about her, once she sets her mind to something, she does it. And right now she's got her mind set on being the best foster parent she can to you. Right?"

"I guess."

"Well, then, I'd say you're stuck with her, because she's not the type to back down." Tyler watched Kevin think that over, hoping his words would make a difference. "In fact, if anything, she's probably worried you aren't going to like her, and that you'll want to end things."

"Really?" Kevin's eyes widened. "I didn't think of that."

"Yup. So try to go easy on her at first anyway, if you can. Like you said, she's new to all this."

"Yeah, I can do that." He stood and went to the dresser, pulling out the contents of the top drawer. "So, are you going to help me or not?"

Dani paced to the front door and peered out the peephole for what might be the hundredth time. As before, the fishbowl view of the front walk showed nothing of interest. Sighing, she told herself to get a grip. They'd be here when they got here. Again, she wished she would have just picked him up, but Tyler had offered to help Kevin pack, and after that it had only made sense to have him bring the kid over. Plus, she had a feeling Kevin might feel more comfortable walking into a new place with Tyler beside him. He'd bonded with the man quickly, and with as much change as he was going through it was good he had someone to lean on.

Heck, Dani wanted to lean on him as well. She felt like a girl waiting for her prom date to show up. Which was silly. But she couldn't help worrying that Kevin wouldn't come, or that he wouldn't like her. What if he hated living with her? Or hated how she'd fixed his room. Maybe she should have left it empty and let him pick things out after he moved in. She'd considered it, but had decided that would be less than welcoming. Now, though, she wondered again if she'd made the right choice. And all that angst was on top of the case of butterflies she got every time she saw Tyler. Her head knew they were just friends, but it hadn't sent the message to the rest of her quite yet.

A knock at the door startled her out of her self-doubt. "Coming!" she called, forcing herself to walk, not run, to let them in.

"Hi," Kevin said shyly, a backpack slung over his shoulder.

"Hi, yourself, kiddo." Dani gave him a brief, one-armed hug, and led the way into the living room. Tyler followed, carrying a suitcase. She almost asked if that was all of it, then bit her tongue. The social worker had told her that foster kids traveled light, many carrying their meager belongings in a plastic trash bag. "Want to put your stuff in your room?"

"Um, sure."

She pointed to the door on the left, opposite her own room. "That's it there. Check it out." Holding her breath, she walked behind and waited for a reaction.

"Oh, my gosh, this is so cool! This is all for me?"

"Of course. If you like it, anyway. If you don't, we can change things up."

"Like it? It's awesome." Starry-eyed, he stood in the middle of the room, turning from side to side to take it all in. She'd chosen a sleek black twin bed with a multicolored striped comforter. A nightstand with a clock radio and a lamp in the shape of a rocket sat next to it, and across the room was a desk, already stocked with paper, pencils and art supplies. Framed posters of popular comic-book heroes hung on the walls, and a funky set of black-and-red shelves held a few books she'd picked up, a stack of comic books and the building toys Tyler had recommended.

"Really?"

Instead of answering, he gave her a hard hug, and then grabbed the suitcase from Tyler. "I'm going to unpack right now."

"Okay, but pizza should be here soon. I figured you'd be hungry and since I wasn't sure what foods you liked, I figured I'd wait and do a big grocery trip tomorrow."

"Pizza's great." He stopped and turned. "Tyler, you're staying for pizza, too, right?"

Tyler shrugged. "I don't know…maybe you and Dani should have time together. Besides, my mom was going to be dropping my girls off at home soon."

"I'm going to be living here—we'll get plenty of time together. Can't you call and ask your mom to drop them off here instead? Please?"

"He's right," Dani insisted. If having Tyler here made the transition easier, then he should stay. "Stay for dinner. I ordered more than enough for us and the twins."

Tyler hesitated, and then nodded. "Okay, but after dinner we've got to go."

Kevin nodded and went back to unpacking, while the adults moved back into the living room.

"You okay with this?" Tyler asked quietly.

"Yeah, I am. It's about making him comfortable."

"Okay then." He pulled out a cell phone and dialed, briefly explaining the change in plans to his mother, before hanging up. "They'll be here in about fifteen minutes, give or take."

"Perfect, the food should be here by then." She headed for the kitchen. "Can I get you a drink? I've got iced tea, juice, milk and water."

"Iced tea would be great."

She took two glasses from the cabinet and filled them with the amber liquid. "What I'd really love is a glass of wine, but it just seems a bit weird to be drinking in front of a kid. Hope you don't mind."

"Not at all. I get your point. I sometimes have a beer while watching a game or something, but I don't want the girls to grow up thinking I have to have a drink every night."

"That makes sense. I guess I'm still just trying to figure things out, you know?"

"So are the rest of us." He leaned a hip against the counter beside her, his hard body just inches from her own. "I think that's really what life's about—feeling your way forward, figuring things out as you go along. There's so much you can't predict. You've just got to be flexible and do the best you can in the moment."

So much of what he said made sense. And there was no doubt that he was talking about more than just tonight, more than just her relationship with Kevin. Part of her wanted to believe what he said. To just let things happen, to live in the moment. Would it be terrible to just see what happened, to take things as they came? Tentatively, she turned toward him, angling herself so they were face-to-face. The heat in his eyes made clear his intentions, and yet instead of backing off, she found herself wanting to let things play out. Her hand itched to reach up and touch him, to feel the hardness of his body and the stubble on his cheek. Could she make a go of it, and still have enough of herself left to take care of Kevin?

Tyler fisted his hands in his pockets. As much as he wanted to take Dani in his arms right there in the kitchen, it wasn't the time or place. But damn, it was hard to remember that when her eyes got all smoky, as if she was thinking the same smoldering thoughts he was. He hadn't intended to seduce her, but it seemed like anytime they were within a few feet of each other the temperature rose about a hundred degrees.

Unable to resist at least one touch of her silky skin, he unclenched one hand to brush her cheek, pushing a wayward strand of hair behind her ear. And then, fingers tingling as if he'd touched a live wire, he forced himself to step away.

"Kevin should be about done in his room," he said, bringing them back to the present just as the doorbell rang.

Dani's eyes widened. Obviously she'd been just as swept up in the moment as him. But she pulled herself together and nodded toward the door. "That's either the pizza or your mother with the girls. If you can get the door, I'll check on Kevin."

"Sure." He watched her walk away, spine straight, lean legs carrying her as if she didn't have a care in the world. But he knew better.

At the door he found his girls, both excited beyond reason over the change in plans. "Grandma says we get to eat pizza, and there is another kid here to play with!" Adelaide shouted, squirming by him to look for either the pizza or the potential new friend. Probably both. Amy hung back, shy in a new situation.

"Thanks, Mom, for watching them today, and for dropping them off. Kevin seems to be settling in, but he wasn't ready for me to leave yet."

"It's no problem. And if anyone can cheer a person up, it's Adelaide. Her enthusiasm will be good for him. Besides, I was hoping to get a glimpse of this lawyer friend of yours."

Tyler groaned inwardly. He should have realized his mother would take this as a matchmaking opportunity, or at least as a chance for some reconnaissance. Pushing her out the door wasn't an option, and before he could think of anything less rude but equally effective, he heard Dani behind him.

"Mrs. Jackson, nice to meet you. I appreciate you bringing the girls over on such short notice."

"Not at all." Donna Jackson stepped forward, forcing Tyler to step aside, and offered her hand to Dani. "I've heard so much about you, I'm glad to finally put a face to the name. I think it's a wonderful thing you're doing, by the way."

"I really don't think—"

"No, it's true. Everyone thinks so, especially Tyler. He's been singing your praises for weeks now."

Dani raised an eyebrow at him, and he shrugged. Maybe he had been talking her up a lot, but he was proud of what she was doing. He may have been hesitant at first, wary of do-gooders who liked to talk about helping but gave up once they realized the hard work involved. But Dani wasn't like that. She wasn't looking for accolades. She was just trying to do the right thing. A habit with her, from what he could tell.

A shriek of laughter brought their attention to the living room, where the girls and Kevin were playing what looked to be some kind of freeze tag involving funny faces and strange poses. Even Amy was smiling as she balanced on one foot, her arms high over her head.

"See, I told you that no one could be tense around Adelaide!" His mom leaned in and gave him a kiss on the cheek, then surprised Dani with a hug. "Don't you worry too much, honey. Kids will have good and bad days, and you just gotta do the best you can to help them through it. But if you need a break, you call me. I love to babysit."

Dani blinked at the sudden show of friendship, then smiled. "Thank you, Mrs. Jackson. I just may take you up on that one of these days."

"Call me Donna. And I hope you do. Have fun, you two." And with a wink she let herself out.

As always, Tyler felt a tug of affection for the woman, laced with a bit of frustration at her need to insert herself into every situation. But he should have expected it. His mother had gone through plenty of hard times herself, raising him as a single parent for a time when his father had been fighting his demons. And then, with the kind of forgiveness he tended to associate with sainthood, she'd welcomed her husband back, once he'd completed a twelve-step program and sworn off the alcohol that had caused their family so much grief. Tyler knew he was lucky to have had such a strong woman to keep hold of him during those rough years. It hadn't been easy; he'd been determined to act out his emotions in pretty self-destructive ways, but she hadn't given up.

And he recognized that same toughness, that same push-through-the-bad-times-and-celebrate-the-good-times attitude, in Dani. He just wished she could see it in herself. Maybe then she'd realize she was strong enough to take on her past, her new life with Kevin and a romance. At least, he hoped that was the case. Because the more he was around her, the less he could imagine a future without her in it.

* * *

Dani finished wrapping up the leftover pizza in foil and placed it in the refrigerator. In the background she heard the water running in the bathroom, hopefully a sign that Kevin was brushing his teeth and getting ready for bed. He'd had a great time at dinner, joking with the young twins and eating his fill. By the time everyone was full, it was getting late, and not long after that Tyler had taken the twins home. Kevin had looked worn out as well, his eyelids drooping as he'd hugged Tyler goodbye. But he hadn't seemed scared or sad, which was what she'd been most worried about.

He had, however, tried to negotiate a later bedtime, an idea she had quickly vetoed. Everything she'd read said that boys his age needed a lot of sleep, given how quickly they were growing. And she knew from experience that a lack of rest could make emotions more difficult to deal with, the last thing he needed as he adjusted to his new living situation. So she'd held firm, and after a few more attempts at negotiation he'd given up. Much to her relief, as she wasn't exactly sure what she would have done if he hadn't. She *really* needed to make time to finish reading the parenting books Tyler had loaned her. Later. After Kevin was in bed, the table was wiped down and she'd gotten some sleep.

"I'm all ready."

Dani turned and found Kevin dressed in a pair of sweatpants and a T-shirt, face clean, teeth hopefully clean, waiting in the living room. Another time she'd ask if he had pajamas, or wanted them. Maybe kids his age were too old for traditional sleepwear? Either way, this would do for now.

"All right, let's get you in bed, kiddo." She walked

with him to his new room, noting that he'd placed a photo of what must have been his mother on the night-stand. That and his backpack were the only personal items she could spot in the room; even the suitcase had left with Tyler, apparently borrowed for the occasion. Again, her heart ached. She knew the Cunninghams had done as much as they could for the boy, and he'd certainly been loved and well fed. But they were living on a fixed income and had taken care of a long list of boys. They could only afford to do so much for each one.

Thankfully her salary, although not impressive by attorney standards, was more than enough to cover the basics for herself and Kevin, as well as some more frivolous things. Not that material items were what mattered, in the end. But right now she was happy she'd picked up the things she had, especially when she saw one of the comic books open on his bed. Moving it carefully to the nightstand she asked, "Is that one good? I wasn't sure what to get, but the store owner said it was popular with kids your age."

Kevin nodded sleepily and climbed onto the bed. "Yeah, it's pretty exciting. I'll probably finish it to-morrow."

"Good, I'm glad. And Kevin?"

"Yeah?"

"I'm glad you're here."

"Me, too." He snuggled down farther under the covers, and then looked up. "Dani, do you think you could keep the door cracked, and the hall light on? Just since it's my first night."

"Sure. Tonight, and any night you want, for as long as you want." Not sure if she should kiss him good-night, or what, she settled for a quick ruffle of his hair, then walked out, being sure to leave the door half-open and the light on.

Once she'd finished cleaning up the kitchen she got into her own pajamas, and curled up in bed with a mug of tea and her laptop. She was nearly as tired as Kevin, but she wanted to check her email and order a night-light for Kevin. Navigating to her favorite online retailer, she found one that looked like the logo from the comic-book brand he seemed to prefer. Perfect. She paid the extra for next-day shipping, then clicked over to her email. Dozens of work emails waited along with a few promotional offers she deleted without reading. Nothing that needed immediate attention. Nothing from Tyler. Not that she'd expected anything—other than arranging things with Kevin, they didn't correspond. Still, after that moment of connection in the kitchen earlier, she'd almost thought he might.

She closed up the computer and set it on the nightstand, then reached for her phone to set the alarm. An icon blinked, showing an unread text message. Clicking on it, she found a short note from Tyler.

Had a great time tonight. Hope Kevin got to bed okay. And Dani, think about what I said in the kitchen.

She bit her lip and then, heart racing, texted back.

Me too. He did. And I will.

She hit Send and tossed the phone back on the nightstand. She hadn't agreed to anything, other than to just think about things. But even that felt huge. If only her fears could be fixed with something as simple as a night-light. Sometimes being the grown-up was hard.

Chapter Nine

"Kevin, wait up!"

Too excited to walk, he slowed from a run to a half trot. Behind him, Dani lengthened her stride, catching up to him just as he climbed the wide, white steps of the historic Sandpiper Inn. Jillian and Nic, the owners, had invited some friends over for a barbecue and although Dani was looking forward to seeing everyone, this would be her and Kevin's first outing as a family. They'd spent the past week working to get into a rhythm with school and work and life, but there were times where she was sure she'd never get the hang of this parenthood thing. And she had a feeling that Kevin had experienced similar moments of doubt.

"Should I knock, like on a house, or just go in, like a hotel?" Kevin looked at her quizzically, one hand poised to rap on the massive door.

"We can just go in, since it is a business and it's daytime hours, but that was a very good question." She paused as a peal of laughter carried on the wind. "Actually, it sounds like everyone is out back. We can just take the porch all the way around." She pointed the way and let him lead. Ironwork tables and well-padded chairs dotted the covered patio, offering inviting spaces for guests to lounge in. Spinning ceiling fans and a large roofed overhang, as well as wise landscaping choices, kept the sheltered porch comfortably cool even at the height of summer. Today, with beautiful spring weather, it was about as perfect a place as she could imagine.

"Hey, there you are! I'm so glad you made it!" Jillian waved from where she was sitting next to Cassie, each with babies on their laps. "Hey, everyone, Dani and Kevin are here."

Everyone had turned out, including their husbands. Nic and Alex, and Alex's sister, Jessica—the three of them were congregated around the grill. And down in the yard, playing catch with Cassie's daughter, Emma, were Tyler and his twins.

"Tyler, what a surprise. I didn't expect you to be here." She looked pointedly at Jillian, who at least had the grace to blush.

"Well, I knew you two were friends, and his girls are about the same age as Cassie's Emma, and…" Jillian trailed off, and Dani found herself laughing at her friend's obvious attempt at matchmaking. No doubt she and Cassie had cooked up the idea together. If Sam hadn't been working this weekend, she'd no doubt be in on the scheme too.

Maybe Dani should be annoyed, but they meant

well. And how could she blame them for thinking there was something going on with her and Tyler, when she'd dreamed about him every night this week? Not to mention all the times she'd texted him, asking for advice or just looking for a word of encouragement. He'd become something important to her, and although she wasn't yet ready to explore the details, she couldn't fault her friends for picking up on it. Or for trying to help it along. So rather than scold them, she gave each woman a hug.

Kevin, already bored with the adult conversation, looked longingly toward the yard below, obviously wanting to join in the game. "Go ahead, go play. Just stay where I can see you, okay?"

"Thanks!"

She watched him nearly tumble down the steps in his haste, letting out a sigh of relief once he had both feet on solid ground. Assured he was happy and safe, she settled into a chair, where she could keep an eye on the kids. "So, how's little Johnny doing, huh?" It always amazed her how much babies could grow and change in such a short period of time.

Jillian shook her head. "Not so little anymore. He's crawling all over the place, and getting into everything. I wouldn't be surprised if he starts walking soon."

"Already?" It was hard to imagine.

"He'll be a year old this summer. I'm trying not to imagine how crazy it's going to be with when the new one gets here. But whenever I say that Nic just laughs and says something about the more, the merrier."

Cassie rolled her eyes, her own baby on her lap. "The guys can say that because they aren't the ones that carry the baby, give birth and breast-feed. I think Alex would have a dozen if he could."

Jillian nodded in understanding. "Exactly. Of course, I'm thrilled to be pregnant again, but it was a bit of a shock. I'd planned to catch up on my sleep a bit before we started all over again. But at least this way they'll be close enough in age to play with each other." She nodded at the children playing below. "How about you, Dani? How are you adjusting to this whole parenting thing?"

"Yeah, I can't imagine it would be easy, to jump in with a kid Kevin's age," Cassie added. "I mean, sure, you get to skip teething, but it seems like there'd be a really steep learning curve."

Dani nodded, not sure what to say. How was she doing? Going for brutal honesty, she laid it out for them. "Honestly, sometimes I think I've got everything figured out, and it's going great. Other times, I'm sure I'm screwing up his life, and he'd be better off with anyone other than me. So I'm not sure what I'm doing is all that fantastic."

Cassie and Jillian exchanged glances, smiling. "I don't know—that sounds pretty typical to me." Cassie pried a lock of her hair out of her infant daughter's chubby hand. "In fact, I'd say you just defined parenting. I swear, just when I think I've got it all figured out, Emma throws me for a loop. Or the baby hits a milestone. Or they're fine, and I end up doubting myself anyway, worried about the future."

"Yup," Jillian agreed. "I mean, I don't have as much experience as Cassie, but that sounds pretty accurate to me."

Dani wasn't sure if she was comforted or appalled by

the idea that what she was going through was normal. Maybe both? "So what you're saying is, I'm never going to figure any of this out?" That was a terrifying thought.

"Yes and no. As time goes on you'll gain more experience and more confidence," Cassie said carefully. "But the truth is, there's no handbook, no one right way to be a parent. All you can do is try to meet their needs, and not drive yourself crazy in the meantime."

Not the kind of advice you'd find cross-stitched on a pillow, but their words made sense. "Well, I seem to be holding on to my sanity. And I think Kevin's doing pretty well, too. It's just a big transition, for both of us."

Tyler, the kids having abandoned him in favor of Jillian's border collie, Murphy, joined them in the shade. "I think you're both doing great. Kevin seems a lot more relaxed than the last time I saw him."

"Really, you think so?" She was starting to think the same, but was afraid it was just wishful thinking.

"I do." His words reassured her, even as his proximity made her stomach jump.

A ruckus from the other end of the patio distracted her, giving her a reason to break eye contact and catch her breath.

"Food's ready," Jessica called from the grill.

"No, it's not," Alex argued, trying to grab the spatula from her hand. "The burgers need a few more minutes."

"They do not. If you cook them any longer, they'll be dry." Evading his grasp, the younger Santiago sibling started transferring the food to a plate.

Tyler shook his head. "If those two are any indication, it seems any hope of my girls outgrowing sibling rivalry is sadly misplaced."

Even as he said it, the twins came up the stairs, pushing to be first in line for the food, with Emma and Kevin right behind them. It warmed her heart to see him fitting in so quickly. Maybe her friends were right; maybe she was doing an okay job of parenting. And if so, did that mean she was ready to tackle the other relationship in her life?

Tyler sank his teeth into his burger and nearly moaned in pleasure. "This might be the best hamburger I've ever had."

"See, I told you so," Jessica gloated, sticking her tongue out at her brother.

"Don't even start," Alex warned. "They're good because we used my recipe, not because a minute would have made a difference one way or another."

"Right, you keep telling yourself that. Besides, it's Mom's recipe, not yours."

"I used it, so it's mine."

"Knock it off, you two." Cassie frowned at her husband. "I'm tired of you two bickering. If Jessica's going to move here and join the department, you two are going to have to learn to get along."

"She's not going to be a cop," Alex growled, eyes narrowed at his little sister, who didn't seem intimidated in the least.

"I am, and there's nothing you can do about it."

Before Alex could respond, Cassie shoved the baby in his arms. "I think Alicia needs a diaper change, if you don't mind." He rolled his eyes at the not so subtle hint, giving his wife a quick kiss of apology before taking the baby into the house.

"Sorry about that," Jessica said sheepishly. "I swear

we normally get along. But I think he was hoping I'd go to grad school after graduating college. Now that I've signed on to join the sherriff's department it's really hit him. He'd rather I do something safer. And from what I can tell, his attitude is pretty common among the men on the force. Things are starting to change, but law enforcement is still a male-dominated world."

"Law, too," Dani agreed. "It's not as bad as it was. There were plenty of women in my law school class, but the partners in the big firms are still almost entirely men. It's a good-old-boys' network, if there ever was one." She took a sip of tea and then paused, before turning back to Jessica again. "You know, if you'd like, we could get together and share some survival strategies about getting ahead in male-dominated professions. I bet we could get my friend Samantha in on it, too. You remember her, the fish-and-wildlife officer? I know she's had an uphill battle as well."

"I'd love that," Jessica said, a light in her eyes. "I'm determined to not let anything stand in my way, but having some strong women at my back can only help. Even if it's just to have someone to complain to who'll understand."

Dani's smile faltered just a bit, and Tyler wondered if she was wondering if things would have worked out differently if she'd had a female mentor to turn to, when she'd first realized she was being harassed. Looking over at the smaller table the kids were sitting at, where they were oblivious to the adult conversation, he thought about the world his daughters were growing up in. It killed him to think that others would use their gender against them, but hopefully, working together, they could make things better in the future. He certainly hoped so.

"I think you should do it. Maybe include other women in the community. From what I know about it, which I admit isn't much, it seems sexual discrimination is something that affects all types of employment, from entry-level positions on up."

"Good point." He could practically see the wheels turning as she thought about the idea. "We could meet at the park, so that women could bring their kids and let them play while we talk."

"I'd go," Cassie said. "Working with my dad, it's not a problem for me now, but I do get clients who think that because I have two X chromosomes I can't possibly know what I'm talking about."

"Go to what?" Alex asked, returning to his seat.

Cassie took the baby back from him so he could start on his food. "It doesn't have a name yet, but Jessica's talking about starting a group for women, where they can discuss sexual discrimination in the workplace." She shot her husband a hard look. "Given how many people still think women can't do the work a man can, I think it's a great idea."

Alex flushed. "Just because I want to keep my baby sister safe doesn't mean I think she isn't capable." Then, looking embarrassed, he turned his attention back to his burger.

The rest of the meal passed in peace, with conversation centering on plans for the upcoming Easter holiday as well as a bit of small-town gossip. He nearly choked when Jillian shared that the senior center, in their never-ending search for fund-raising ideas, was talking about holding a Ms. Senior Citizen pageant, complete with a bathing-suit competition. By the time everyone finished giving their take on that, everyone's plates were empty and the sun was starting to set.

Nic stood and called over to the kids' table, "Who wants to roast marshmallows for dessert?"

Of course they all did, so Nic and Alex went to start up a fire in the fire pit, with the kids in tow. Jillian rose, a sleepy-eyed baby on her shoulder. "I'm going to go see if I can get Johnny to sleep. Cassie, if you want to lay Alicia down, you can use the playpen in the master bedroom."

"Thanks, I think I will."

While the two mothers went inside, Jessica started clearing the table. Dani started to help, but Jessica shooed her away. "I've got this. You two relax. From what Cassie tells me, parents don't get to do much of that."

Dani hesitated. "Are you sure?"

"Definitely. When this is done, I get the rest of the night off. You two will have kids on a sugar high to deal with. I'm getting the better end of this bargain, trust me."

Before Dani could argue anymore, Tyler pulled her away. "She's right. Come on, we've probably got five, ten minutes before the kids start asking us to help them put the marshmallows on the sticks. Let's enjoy it while we can." Dani let Tyler steer her to a cushioned porch swing and tried to let go of any guilt over not helping out Jessica. Like Tyler said, her reprieve was sure to be short-lived, and this was the first time since Kevin moved in that she'd had a moment to just slow down and relax.

Tyler joined her on the swing, putting it in motion

with a gentle push. "So," he said after a moment, "I asked you last week to think about what I said. About being open to possibilities?"

She nodded cautiously.

"And have you thought about it?"

Only in every spare moment. "I have."

"And?"

"And I'm terrified and overwhelmed and have no idea what the right thing to do is." She took a breath, needing to say the rest before she chickened out. "But I think I need to at least figure it out, figure out what is going on with us."

Tyler let out a breath. "Can I say now how scared I was that you were going to tell me to shove off?"

She laughed. "Hey, I still might. I'm not committing to anything. I still want to take it one step of a time, one day at a time." Hell, one minute at a time.

"I'm not asking for anything else." He shifted, taking her hand in both of hers. It was the kind of touch that spoke more of solidarity than foreplay, but still her pulse reacted. "And if at any point I do anything that makes you uncomfortable or go too far, I want you to promise to tell me."

"I will." She gripped his hand, feeling the solidity behind it. "I talked to my therapist about us."

"Really?"

"Really. I told her about being attracted to you, and that we'd been…well, that we'd kissed, and been physical." She felt her cheeks heat. "And that I had enjoyed it."

"Me, too."

"But I also told her about my panic attack." They'd discussed it a great deal, actually. "And you should know, she thinks it could happen again. I don't know that it will, but it might."

"And if it does, we'll deal with it. Whatever that means."

"You don't think that's weird, that I could freak out at any random moment, even when we're being intimate?" Hell, she thought it was weird, and she was the one living it.

He traced his thumb across her wrist, reigniting the sparks that seemed to flare whenever they touched. "No. Given what you've been through, it seems perfectly natural. The only thing I'm worried about is me making it worse. If I'm going to get in the way of the progress you're making, I'll step back until you give me the okay."

She shook her head, marveling again at his selflessness. "You make it better, not worse. I feel safe with you." And she did. It didn't make any sense at all, but being near him, touching him, grounded her and helped her to think more clearly, to see things as they really were without the fog of fear clouding her mind. Maybe it was him; maybe it was seeing that she could be around him and not freak out that made her feel better. Either way, she liked it.

"That's good." He leaned in closer. "But I'd like to think I inspire some other feelings, too."

She shivered, his voice tickling its way through her body. "Oh, you do." Right now several were competing for attention, with lust leading the pack.

Rather than replying, he dipped his head, pressing a quick, heated kiss to her lips. Startled, and wanting more, she started to reach for him.

"Honey, I'd love to do more than that, but I think our time's about up."

Sure enough, the sound of sneaker-clad feet pounding up the steps signaled the return of the kids. Adelaide, as usual, was in the lead. "Daddy, the fire's ready! Can we have marshmallows now?"

Tyler let out an *oomph* as both his girls jumped into his lap. "How do you ask?"

"Please?" the twins said in unison.

"I suppose. Let's see if Jillian has some roasting sticks for us to use."

"She does," Emma assured him. "I heard her say she was bringing them out. She's got graham crackers and chocolate, too, for s'mores."

"Can I make some, too?" Kevin asked, looking hopefully at Dani.

"Of course you can. But I'm warning you, s'mores are my favorite. I might eat them all up before you get any."

"No way!"

"We'll see," she said with a wink. It was so good to see Kevin laughing and having a good time. He'd had way too few evenings like this in his short life. Even before his mother died, life had been hard. The social worker had filled her in—money had been tight, and there hadn't been time or funds for extras. Then, when his mom had gotten cancer, the situation spiraled down fast. From what she'd learned, his mother had done an admirable job of sheltering Kevin as much as she could from the stress she was under, but he was a sensitive boy. He would have known. And foster care, even in the best of circumstances, had added a whole new layer of stress. And she counted herself in that category. No matter how good her intentions were, a new living situation meant new stress for the boy. Her parenting class had warned about spoiling a child in a misguided attempt to make up for the guilt, but they had meant over-the-top presents and such. Her gut told her that a small outing with friends, making s'mores, could only be good for him.

A bag of marshmallows, several bars of chocolate and more graham crackers than she could remember later, and she was sure of it—s'mores were good therapy. And not just for Kevin. She was feeling more relaxed than she had in ages. And why shouldn't she feel good? She had wonderful friends who cared about her, an incredibly attractive man interested in her and the boy she was coming to love was smiling and content. Add in the stars overhead and the smell of orange blossoms on the breeze, and it made for a perfect night. Leaning back in one of the camp chairs Nic had set out, she found herself wishing they could do this every night.

Mirroring her thoughts, Kevin shook the empty marshmallow bag, and then looked wistfully at the fire as he asked, "When can we do this again?"

"Well, roasting marshmallows isn't exactly an everyday thing. You do it on special occasions, like a cookout with friends, or when you are camping."

"Can we go camping?" Kevin's face, illuminated by the fire, nearly glowed on its own with sheer excitement. "I've never been. But some of the guys at school were talking about going. They slept in tents, and ate hot dogs, and even saw raccoons getting into their trash." Coming closer, he knelt in front of her chair, eyes pleading. "Please, please, please, can we go camping?"

Dani balked. Sleeping on the ground? Cooking on a fire? Raccoons? "Um…I guess? I've never been camping, either, Kevin, so I'm not sure I would even know what to do."

"You've never been camping? How is that possible?" Tyler looked at her, amazed.

"My sister is the outdoorsy one. I like modern conveniences. Campfires notwithstanding, of course."

"It's true," Cassie said, backing her up. "Mollie's a wildlife photographer, and happiest on a boat or out in the marsh. It's hard to believe they're even sisters sometimes."

"You're missing out then. The Paradise Wildlife Refuge has great camping facilities and it's practically in your backyard. The girls and I go several times a year, don't we?"

"Uh-huh." Amy nodded. "I have my very own sleeping bag. It has a princess on it."

"And we can get as dirty as we want when we're camping," Adelaide added.

"You know, it sounds like you three are experts," Jillian said speculatively. "I bet Dani and Kevin could really benefit from your experience. Maybe you should do a group trip?"

"Yes! Daddy, let's do it, please?"

"Please, Daddy? I used the magic word and asked nicely this time, so you have to say yes."

"Saying 'please' is the polite thing to do, but it doesn't mean I have to say yes. It's not a guarantee. I think Dani and Kevin need to decide if they want other people on their trip."

"Of course we do." Kevin looked up expectantly. "Don't we, Dani?"

Jillian had done it again. She was going to have to have a word with her friend about matchmaking. But right now, she had three children staring at her as if she held the keys to the kingdom. And really, if she had to go camping, it would be nice to have someone along who knew what they were doing. And could scare raccoons away. "Fine, yes. That would be great. If it works for Tyler, of course. He may not be free for a while."

"Actually, I'm free next weekend. And if we're going to do this, we should go before the weather gets too hot. It's miserable in the summer."

"Awesome!" Kevin hugged her, and she briefly felt like she'd done something really right.

Then she thought about spending a long, moonlit night in the middle of nowhere with Tyler. By a fire, with the children fast asleep. And wondered if her take-it-slow plan had just been thrown into fast forward.

Chapter Ten

Putting up a tent wasn't that hard. Unless you had two little girls who were "helping" you do it. Then it was next door to impossible. Dani and Kevin, despite their inexperience, were having much better luck. They were driving in the last stake of their borrowed tent and he was still trying to sort out the poles that his girls kept rearranging.

"Done!" Kevin grinned triumphantly. "That was fun."

Fun wasn't the word Tyler would choose. "Hey, girls, Kevin and Dani have their tent up. Maybe you two should go check it out."

"Okay!" Adelaide bounced away, dragging her sister behind her.

"Need some help?" Dani walked up and eyed the tangle of gear.

"I think what I actually need is a little less help. At least from the five-and-under set."

"Gotcha. Want me to keep them busy while you finish up here?"

"That would be great. Thanks."

"Anytime."

Turning back to the job at hand, he quickly sorted out the parts, snapped the poles together and inserted them into the proper sleeves on the tent. Not hard, as long as you didn't have someone grabbing at them, begging to do it themselves. Normally he didn't mind the extra time it took, but right now every second he spent wrangling his gear was a second he wasn't spending with Dani.

Dani, who, in her khaki shorts and red tank top, had his more primal instincts stirring. He'd give anything for a few minutes alone with her, but for now he'd settle for sharing her with the kids. All of whom were just as fascinated by her as he was. Kevin had blossomed in the few short weeks he'd been living with her, thriving on the attention and affection she provided. And Amy and Adelaide were equally charmed, hanging on her every word. They seemed to come alive around her, laughing and smiling more than before. Maybe they just missed having a woman around, but it seemed like more than that. Dani just had that effect on everyone, including him.

And he wasn't missing out on one minute more. Dusting his hands off on his jeans, he ducked into her dome-style tent and whistled. They'd strung it up well and had their sleeping bags and gear stowed neatly. "Looks good. Are you sure you guys haven't done this before?"

"Nope." Kevin shook his head.

"It's just that we have good gear. Thankfully my sister has everything anyone could ever need when it comes to outdoor equipment, and keeps it stored down here even when she's in Atlanta."

"Good gear does make it easier," he agreed. "But you two worked well together. You make a good team."

Dani smiled and gave Kevin a high five. "We do, don't we?"

"What about us, are we a good team?" Amy's brow furrowed. "You put the tent up without us."

"Of course we're a good team. You two organized the poles for me, remember?" He winked at Dani. "The Three Musketeers, that's us."

"Now we're the Five Musketeers, with Dani and Kevin," Adelaide corrected. "We can all be a team together."

"You're right. My mistake. And I think the first thing this team should do is to explore. Who wants to learn how to use a compass?"

As he expected, everyone was interested. He'd brought some small children's compasses from the shop, and as expected each kid wanted his or her own to use. Crouching down, he showed them how to line the needle up with north, and then use that to see which way they were facing. Once they had the hang of it, he started calling out directions. "Twelve paces east. Good, now ten paces south. Turn to the west. Take five steps." He continued to direct them for another few minutes, trying not to laugh at their inexpert attempts at navigation. The children ran in to each other a few times as they worked out which way was which, but eventually all of them were where he'd specified. "Good. Now look in the hollow of that tree."

"Chocolate!" Adelaide yelled, pulling out three large bars from where he'd hidden them earlier.

Amy hugged a bag to her chest. "And marshmallows!"

Which left Kevin retrieving the box of graham crackers. "Does this mean we get to make s'mores?"

"I guess we have to. You all earned it. But first, we need to build the campfire and get dinner going. Then dessert."

"I've got the fire under control, if you'll get the dinner fixings out," Dani called from where she crouched over the grill pit.

"What? When did you do that?" He had fully anticipated having to do that job himself, given her lack of outdoors experience.

She smiled smugly. "While you and the kids were doing your treasure hunt. Before we came I watched some videos on the internet, and it seemed pretty simple. So I gave it a try."

Impressed, he walked over and checked out her work. A classic cooking fire, with a crisscross construction, perfectly executed. "You really are amazing, you know that?"

"Because I can follow directions? Like I said, it wasn't that hard, once I knew what to do."

"No, because you didn't let being in a new situation intimidate you. You used it as an opportunity to educate yourself, and despite being out of your element, gave it your best shot. And succeeded, I should add. That's impressive. Not many people would have made that effort."

"What, did you think I was going to leave all the outdoorsy stuff to you, while I sat in a chair and observed from a distance?"

He shrugged guiltily. He had kind of expected that, but he realized now he shouldn't have. She wasn't one to back away from a challenge, real or perceived. She'd agreed to go camping, so despite her personal uneasiness, she'd tackled camping the way she did everything else, wholeheartedly and without reservations. Just like she'd done with Kevin. Lack of experience obviously wasn't an excuse, not in her world. It was an attitude that was not only refreshing, but also infectious. Being with her made him think anything was possible. And that was a feeling he hadn't had in a long, long time.

Dani wasn't sure which tasted better, the gooey marshmallow in her mouth or sweet success. She'd not only managed to set up a tent, but she'd also started a fire and cooked over it. And so far, no raccoons! Even better, the kids had all been so exhausted from the fresh air and sunshine that they had passed out early. Now the moon was rising, the stars were shining and she was sitting by a fire she'd built herself with a man that was capturing her heart a bit more every day.

He'd been amazing with the kids earlier, teaching them patiently and truly having fun with them. It was obvious he didn't just tolerate children; he sincerely enjoyed being around them.

Of course, that made sense for a man who ran a toy store for a living, but it was a welcome shift from some of the men she'd met before. Most of them had felt that earning a paycheck was the only contribution they needed to make, and left the hands-on parenting to their wives or, even better, a nanny. Looking back at the high-pressure corporate law environment she'd left, she said a small prayer of gratitude. Not for the way things had happened, but for whatever reason she'd ended up back in Paradise. This was the place she loved, and these were the kinds of people she wanted to be around. They worked hard, but they also made time for family and friends. And, it seemed, for romantic relationships.

Tyler watched her as she finished eating, his eyes reflecting the firelight. "Was it as good as the look on your face makes it seem?"

"Oh, yeah." She licked a bit of sticky sugar from her lip and watched his jaw twitch. "Want a taste?"

"I thought you'd never ask." Leaning in, he nibbled at her lip. "Mmm…sweet. Have I mentioned how good you taste?"

"You mean the marshmallow." She kissed him back, hard and fast.

"No, I mean you." This time he kissed her more thoroughly, using his tongue, teeth and lips to tease and torment, assailing her senses until the heat between them burned hotter than the fire itself. Needing more, she slid her hands under his shirt, feeling the hard strength that should scare her, but didn't. When he moved from her mouth to her neck, she arched, digging her nails into his skin.

This time, it was his hands that explored, trailing up and down her side before skimming beneath her tank top. His mouth tickled her skin as she spoke. "I want to lay you down by the fire and peel your clothes off, one by one, until I can see every inch of you by the glow of the firelight." She shivered, knowing that if the children weren't so close at hand she'd let him; no, she'd beg him to do exactly that. Instead, she angled her head back toward him, seeking his mouth, needing to show him how she felt with her kiss.

Minutes passed as they rode the rise and fall of passion, each careful not to push too far as they explored each other's reactions. Never had she felt so cared for, so cherished. At no point did she feel like Tyler was using her for his own satisfaction; instead every touch, every moment, was another attempt to bring her pleasure. When Tyler finally pulled back, a look of wonder on his face, she nearly dragged him back against her, protesting. But then he placed a finger against her newly swollen lips, shushing her.

"What?" she mumbled against his finger, frustrated.

"Look," he whispered, pointing past her.

At first all she saw was the picnic table, nearly hidden in the shadows of the pines surrounding the campsite. Then a movement caught her eye. There, climbing onto the far bench, looking for leftovers, was one of the masked bandits she'd heard so much about. "Raccoons?" She kept her voice low, not sure if loud noises would scare them off, which would be good, or provoke them to attack. Not so good.

"Yep. They'll leave once they realized we didn't leave them any snacks."

Dani gripped his hand and watched, equal parts terrified and fascinated, as the furry creatures explored every nook of the space they'd eaten at just a few hours ago. "They won't try to get in the tents, will they?" She shifted her attention to the two domes where the children slept.

"No, they don't like people. Just our food."

"Good." She'd defend Kevin and the girls with her life if she had to, but she'd rather just snuggle by the fire. Shifting, she leaned back onto Tyler's broad chest, telling herself to relax even as she kept a wary eye on the raccoons. Sure enough, after a thorough inspection of the campsite the intruders waddled off, noses sniffing the air, searching for better prospects.

Dani sighed, the last bit of tension melting away. Tyler wrapped his arms around her, warming her with his body. "This is nice." And it was, all of it. The firelight, the sounds of nature and, most of all, Tyler.

"It is. We should make it a habit."

"Camping?"

"No." He nuzzled her neck, making her squirm against him. "I mean this. Snuggling. Kissing. Touching."

"Oh."

"You don't think so?"

She hesitated, struggling to put her thoughts into words. "It's not that I don't want to. I do. But as much fun as this is, and as much as I want to keep doing this, I need you to promise me something."

"Is this about your PTSD? Because I told you, I'll never push you. You set the limits."

"No, it's not about that."

"Then what?"

"I need you to promise that no matter what happens with us, the kids come first."

"Of course." He answered quickly, easily.

She turned, twisting until she was facing him head-on. "I'm serious, Tyler. I want to believe that I can handle being a foster parent, a single mom, and also a romantic relationship. I do. But if I can't, if something has to give, it can't be Kevin. He has to be my first priority."

"Of course he is. I wouldn't expect any different."

"That means I may not always have time for you, at least not as much as you, or I, would like. Between work and Kevin, there may not be a lot of time left over to build a relationship."

"That's okay, I can be very efficient." He kissed the nape of her neck, making her want to forget all about priorities. But she couldn't.

"Tyler, I'm serious."

"So am I. For instance, I'm pretty sure I could have both of us naked in less than a minute if I really tried." She sighed, and he grinned. "Okay, so maybe that's not what you meant. But Dani, both of us are adults. We aren't going to get our feelings hurt if one of us has to cancel a date because of a sick kid, or blow off dinner in order to work on a school project. If anything, I think we're better together, and I think our kids feel the same way. But I promise, if anything changes, and it comes down to either the kids or our relationship, they win. No question."

A weight lifted off her shoulders at his words. She wanted this to work, more now than ever, but she refused to go into it blind. But as long as they were both on the same page, she was willing to believe they had a chance. That maybe dreams could come true, even ones you didn't know you had.

Dani woke to sunlight streaming in through the tent and the smell of coffee brewing. Heaven. Rolling over, she checked on Kevin and saw he was still fast asleep, tucked deeply into his sleeping bag. No need to wake him—maybe she could even get some caffeine in her before he was up and raring to go. She'd slept in sweats, so didn't have to change before leaving the tent. Just a quick run of a brush through her hair would do it.

Outside, the campground was quiet, with the muted sounds of breakfast preparations filtering through the trees. At their own little spot, the fire was blazing, with an old-fashioned percolator heating on the grate. Sitting in a camp chair, long legs stretched out in front of him, was Tyler, looking even better than the coffee smelled. And that was saying something. A morning person she wasn't, especially after sleeping on the ground.

"Hey, beautiful. Sleep well?"

"Nope." She smiled. "But that's okay. I'm here for the company, not the accommodations."

He reached out and took her hand, pulling her down for a quick kiss before reaching for the coffeepot. He filled a blue enamel mug with the steaming brew and passed it over to her. "I've got cream and sugar on the picnic table if you want it."

"Normally yes, but honestly I want caffeine too much to be picky right now." She took a sip of the pungent brew and nearly choked. "Then again, maybe I will." She walked over to the table and doctored her cup.

"Sorry, I should have warned you. Campfire coffee tends to be a bit on the strong side."

"Strong like jet fuel. At least it should wake me up."

"If it doesn't, I've got a few thoughts on how we could accomplish that." He waggled his eyebrows, drawing a reluctant laugh from her at his antics.

"I'll keep that in mind." Not that she'd mind a little of what he was suggesting, but she wasn't delusional enough to think the kids would be asleep much longer. Sure enough, even as she thought it, Tyler's tent door unzipped, revealing two little girls with bad cases of bed head.

"Well, there are my two favorite camp girls. How are you this morning?"

"Hungry," pouted Adelaide.

"And thirsty," added Amy. "I want orange juice."

"Sorry," Tyler said, scooping up a girl in each arm. "They aren't morning people. They'll turn into humans once they get some food in them."

"No problem. I'm on their side."

He dropped the girls on the picnic bench and rummaged in the cooler, coming up with two juice boxes. He placed one in front of each, then brought out another and set it on the other side. "For Kevin, once he wakes up. Do you want one, too?"

She shook her head. "I'm good with coffee, thanks. Want some help with breakfast?"

"Nah, you made dinner, I'll handle this. Besides, it seems as the designated morning person, it's my duty to feed the rest of you night owls."

"Thanks." Settling into the surprisingly comfortable camp chair, she watched him mix up pancakes and then pour them into perfect circles on a griddle he'd brought for the fire. Sausage links followed, and in less time than it took her to finish her first cup of coffee he had a full breakfast cooked up. She stood, and headed for the tent. "I'll go wake Kevin. I know he's tired but he won't forgive us if he misses a meal."

She found him sitting up, fully dressed, with his

sleeping bag already rolled up and stowed in its bag. "Wow, you've been busy. Come on out and join us—Tyler made pancakes."

He didn't answer, but followed silently, sitting down across from the twins. It wasn't like him to be so quiet, but maybe he was still sleepy. Dani plated up the pancakes for everyone while Tyler finished cooking the last batch, then sat down to eat herself. "So, how are they?" she asked before digging in.

"Good!" Amy said around a mouthful.

"Yummy. I love pancakes and sausages," Adelaide agreed.

Kevin just shrugged and continued eating, his eyes on his plate.

"What do you think, Kevin, you like my cooking?" Tyler sat next to him with his own giant stack of flapjacks.

"It's fine."

Tyler glanced over at Dani in surprise. She shrugged, at a loss herself to explain the less than enthusiastic response. He hadn't done anything rude, exactly, but he was certainly in a very different mood from last night. If it continued, she'd ask him about it. In the meantime, they needed to finish eating, and then break camp. Tomorrow was a school day, and she wanted to get home in time to do some laundry and get organized.

After breakfast she and Tyler cleaned up while the kids played. Or rather, Amy and Adelaide picked fights with each other and Kevin watched.

"What do you think is up with Kevin?" she asked, handing Tyler the syrup to put in the cooler.

"He's probably upset about leaving. Even the girls

are cranky about it. They'd stay out here for a week if we could."

"I hope that's all it is. He's just acting really strangely."

"I'm sure it is." He put the last of the supplies in his car, then scanned the campsite. "Want some help taking down your tent?"

"No, you get yours. I can handle mine with some help from Kevin."

As it turned out, she had to handle it alone, because Kevin was all but useless. He scuffed his feet, struggled to untie lines and basically did as little as possible. Finally, more frustrated by him than the tent, she sent him to play with the twins. Thankfully, taking it down was easier than putting it up, and other than having to refold it three times to make it fit in the bag, it went smoothly.

Tyler had already finished packing up his car and was rounding up the kids by the time she finished.

Adelaide stomped her foot on the pine-needle-covered ground. "Do we have to go home already?"

Frowning, Amy stood behind her, arms crossed in silent agreement.

"Yes, we do. For one thing, we ate all the food. And as cranky as you girls are already, I'm not sticking around to see what happens once you get hungry."

Kevin listened from a distance, then walked to where Dani had her smaller car parked beside Tyler's and got in. No argument from him, at least. She didn't envy Tyler the drive home with the twins. He managed to get them buckled into their booster seats, and then, a frazzled expression on his face, instructed them not to fight with each other or he'd leave them for the bears.

Dani laughed at the girls' mock shrieks of terror.

Yes, they were sad to be leaving, but truth be told, so was she. Not that camping was likely to become her new favorite pastime, but it had been heaven having so much time with Tyler. Now they were returning to their own hectic lives, and making room for each other wouldn't be easy.

"I'm going to miss you," he said, stepping in close where they were out of view of the children.

"Same. But we'll see each other soon, right?"

"Right." He sounded confident, but they both knew it would be difficult. Still, she'd agreed to try to make things work between them, and so they'd just have to find a way. "And until then, maybe this will hold you over." He pulled her to him and, with ruthless precision, proceeded to give her the best kiss she'd ever had, primitive but effective. Then, as if he hadn't nearly reduced her to a puddle of hormones, he loped off to his car and drove away.

"Wow." She whispered the word, then put a hand to her still tingling lips. Yeah, she'd remember that, all right. She'd be lucky if she could think of anything else.

Chapter Eleven

"Kevin, you need to get up! You're going to be late for school." She turned on the overhead light, hoping maybe that would get him to stir. She'd already tried waking him up twice and time was getting short.

"Okay. I'm getting up. You don't have to yell." He kicked the covers off and sat up, glaring at her.

"I didn't yell. I was just…never mind. Just hurry up please. I put a yogurt and some toast on the table for you. There isn't time for anything else." Leaving him to get ready, she went and finished her own preparations for the day. She'd already dried her hair, happy as always that the short bob was so quick to style, but she still needed to apply her makeup. She didn't wear much, but a bit of color on her cheeks, some eyeliner and a touch of lipstick never hurt anybody.

Back in the main part of the house she found Kevin,

dressed for school and picking at his food. Sleepy and cranky she could understand, but not wanting to eat? Something was up.

"Are you feeling okay?" She put her hand to his forehead the way she remembered her own mother doing to her. He didn't seem hot. She'd chalked up yesterday's behavior to exhaustion and being upset about the camping trip being over. But if that was the case, why was he still out of sorts? "Is your stomach upset or something?"

He shook his head and took a token bite of toast.

"Okay. Well, if anything is bothering you, anything at all, you can tell me, okay?"

He nodded but didn't meet her gaze. Where was the happy child of last week, the one that talked a mile a minute and wolfed down twice as much food as she did? "Seriously, Kevin, I mean it. If something's wrong, I want to help."

"I'm fine. Just leave me alone, okay?" He took a last bite of toast, leaving most of the food on his plate. "Didn't you say we were late? Let's just go."

Startled by his burst of temper, she thought about insisting they talk things out, right here, right now. But the look on his face said she'd be unlikely to make much headway. And he was right: they *were* running late. Frustrated, she grabbed her briefcase and purse, and headed for the door. "Fine. We can deal with this later."

Looking relieved, Kevin picked up his backpack from its spot by the front door and followed her out. He didn't say another word the entire drive to school, and when she told him goodbye as he got out of the car he ignored her, stalking off without a word.

Stunned and hurt, she sat there staring after him until the car behind her honked in annoyance. School drop-off lines were not known for being tolerant of slowpokes. "Fine, I'm moving, I'm moving." She waved in apology and navigated her way out of the parking lot, mindful of any children that might dart out in front of her. Once out on the main road she relaxed the death grip she'd taken on the steering wheel and told herself to chill out. *He's a kid. He's going to do things that seem rude, and he's going to be moody sometimes. He's been through a lot. This is probably normal.*

All of which was true. Except she knew Kevin, and this wasn't like him. He might have only moved in a short time ago, but she'd been working with him for months as his guardian *ad litem*, and this wasn't anywhere near typical behavior for him. Which meant something was bothering him, but what?

Was he having regrets about her fostering him? Was he maybe jealous that he'd had to share the weekend with Tyler and the twins instead of having her all to himself? But that didn't make sense, either; he'd been thrilled about having them there. If anything, he'd welcomed having another guy on the trip. And as much as the twins were on the young side, he always seemed to enjoy playing with them. It gave him a chance to be the older, bigger kid, to show off some leadership skills, and he seemed to like that.

So that didn't make sense, but neither did anything else. And that scared the crap out of her. She was his foster mother, and moms were supposed to be able to fix things. How could she fix it if she didn't even know what the problem was? And why wouldn't he just tell her? She'd thought they had a close relationship, that he trusted her. Respected her, even. But the way he'd been behaving in the last twenty-four hours made it seem like he didn't care about her at all.

Could she really have read him so wrong? And if so, what the heck was she supposed to do about it? She couldn't force him to talk. And she certainly wasn't doing a great job of figuring it out on her own. All she could do was hope he'd either work out what was bothering him, or trust her enough to tell her about it. Both required patience, not a particularly strong trait of hers.

But like it or not, there was nothing she could do right now. Pulling into the office parking lot, she forced herself to switch from parent mode to work mode. Kevin wasn't the only one counting on her; her clients were, too. And at least with them she was confident she'd be able to help. If only kids were as easy to figure out as the law.

"What'll it be this morning, Tyler?" Grace Keville, the owner and proprietress of the Sandcastle Bakery, asked as she grabbed a cellophane bag. He made a habit out of stopping here on Mondays, his weekly morning off, and she knew he had a sweet tooth.

"Two tangerine scones, and two cups of coffee please. Cream and sugar in both."

"Two?" She raised a brow.

"I'm bringing breakfast to a…friend." He wasn't sure how public Dani wanted their relationship to be at this point. Better to ask her first before broadcasting it around town. That is, if the goofy smile on his face wasn't already doing that.

"And would that friend be a lady lawyer, here in town?"

He shook his head. "The news is already out, huh?"

She winked, then set about filling his order. "This is Paradise, remember? I'm sure most of the town knew before you did." She handed him a drink holder with two steaming cups of fragrant coffee, with the bag of scones nestled between them. "If it helps, everyone is highly supportive of the relationship."

"Well, that's better than the alternative, anyway." He paid the bill and put a generous tip in the jar. "Have a good morning."

"You, too, and say hi to Dani for me."

"I will."

He left the shop and headed for the small law office Dani and her father shared. Housed on the first floor of a pale stucco building, it was located between a custom framing shop and a personal accountant. Pushing open the heavy, wooden door, he found himself in a small but elegantly appointed reception area. Hardwood floors, vaulted ceilings and an antique desk gave it an old-world feel. Upholstered chairs were positioned around a glossy oak coffee table strewn with current magazines. Soft classical music played in the background, obscuring the traffic noises from outside.

"Hello, can I help you?"

Sitting at the front desk was an older, more matronly version of Dani. The hair color wasn't the same, but the smile was, and that was enough to make him instantly like her.

"I hope so. I'm looking for Dani."

"And you are?"

"Tyler. Tyler Jackson."

A knowing look passed over her face. "I thought so. Well, it's nice to meet you, Tyler. I've heard a lot about you."

"You have?" Somehow he hadn't imagined Dani would have said much about him, or their relationship.

"Oh, not from Dani." She grinned. "She doesn't like to talk about her personal life. But I have other sources."

Of course. The Paradise Isle gossip brigade strikes again. Unsure what to say, he gave what he hoped was a noncommittal shrug.

"She's in her office. First door on the left."

"Thank you."

He found Dani typing away at her desk, a heavy book of some sort open beside her laptop. Her eyes darted back and forth between the book and the screen, her face a study in concentration. Only when he set down the coffee and scones on her desk did she notice his presence.

"Tyler! What are you doing here?"

"Bringing breakfast to a beautiful woman, obviously."

Her cheeks pinkened as she reached for the bakery bag. "Shouldn't you be at work instead of playing delivery boy?" She took a big bite of the decadent pastry and then shook her head. "Forget I said that. I don't care where you were supposed to be—this scone is worth it. Yum."

He fished the other one out of the bag and sat in the chair across from her desk. "I usually take Monday mornings off. I've got a clerk that comes in so I can run errands and such without dragging the girls with me. That way, weekends can be for family time, instead of going to the grocery store and the post office."

She nodded over the rim of her coffee cup. "That makes sense. I've been rushing to try to get things done on my lunch hour, but it's been hard." She took another sip and set down the cup with a sigh. "Actually, everything feels hard right now.

"What do you mean?"

"It's Kevin. He's still acting strangely. Like he can't stand to be around me. He didn't even say goodbye this morning when I dropped him off. Something isn't right and I have no idea what it could be. And I should know. It's my job to know."

"Hey, you're not a mind reader. If he won't talk about it, you just have to be patient. Give him some time, and let him know you're there for him."

"I'm doing that. At least, I think I am. It's hard to tell. I just feel like I should be better at this than I am."

"You're doing fine. It's not like kids come with an instruction manual."

She rolled her eyes at him. "Says the man who owns a stack of parenting books."

She had him there. "I didn't say I hadn't tried to figure it all out. But as good as those books are, they can't tell you everything. And they don't know Kevin. You do. If you think something is off, go with your gut. Keep an eye on him, and let him know you'll listen if he has something to say. He'll come around. And you know, it may have nothing to do with you at all. He could have a crush on a girl at school or something. Who knows?"

"Maybe." She rubbed her temples, and he saw the

tight pinch of pain in her eyes. "But in the meantime I've given myself a tension headache worrying about it."

"Here, let me help."

He stood and walked around the desk to stand behind her. He placed his hands on her shoulders and kneaded the tight muscles. "You know another thing that helps ease tension?"

She shook her head, her soft hair brushing against the backs of his hands. Leaning down, he gently kissed her right where her shoulder curved to meet her neck. "A little fooling around."

Dani stiffened, every muscle locking up. Dear God, not again. But like it or not, it was happening. Her heart pounded as her body screamed at her to get up and run. Except she couldn't move; she was frozen in place, panting in fear.

Vaguely, she heard Tyler say her name, but she couldn't focus on what he was saying. Instead, she closed her eyes, shutting him and everything out, the way her therapist had taught her. Focus on her breathing: that was the biggest thing. In and out, slowly, counting to four with each inhalation, then exhaling to eight. Letting the sound and feel of the air moving through her lungs remind her that she was okay. Nothing bad was happening. She was safe. In and out. She focused on being safe, on being in the present.

When her pulse stopped throbbing in her ears, she took a chance and opened her eyes. Tyler was leaning against the wall a few feet away, concern furrowing his brow, hands stuffed deep in his pockets. He'd taken as unthreatening a stance as possible while keeping her in his sight. She'd have to thank him for that later. First she needed a drink of water. She kept a water bottle in her bag, next to her chair. Grabbing it, she drank deeply. Panic attacks always left her thirsty, as if she'd just run a marathon rather than fought her own mind.

"Are you okay now? Is it over?" Tyler kept his position against the wall, but she could tell he wanted to move closer. That he didn't, despite his instincts, gave her the warm fuzzies. Some women liked jewelry. It seemed her big soft spot was for a man who knew how to handle her anxiety. Sad, but true.

"Yeah, it's better now. That wasn't a bad one. It just took me by surprise."

"Me, too. I figured, after the other times, you'd be okay."

She nodded soberly. "Two steps forward, one step back."

"Hey, that's still a net gain." He grinned, obviously trying to cheer her up.

"I guess so. I just like the moving-forward part a lot better."

"Me, too. Any idea what it was, what I did, that triggered it?"

"Not really… I always thought it was just being near men in general, but obviously that's not usually the case with you."

"Well, then, something was different. I startled you earlier, and you already had a headache. Maybe it was just bad timing."

"Maybe." Hormones, mood, any of that could have an effect on PTSD. "Or it could be where we are."

"Your office?" Understanding lit his face. "You mean an office, in general. Maybe your desk, in particular."

"Exactly. Right before you kissed me, I was looking down at my desk, and I could see my laptop and that obnoxious book of case law out of the corner of my eye. The same things I probably had on my desk, more or less, in Jacksonville, when the attack happened." She forced herself to say "attack" and not "incident." Her therapist had insisted she call it what it was and not allow her subconscious to minimize it. Something about needing to face it consciously in order to stop her subconscious mind from carrying the burden.

"That makes sense. Being startled probably triggered your stress hormones, which were already high because of your worry about Kevin. Then I kissed you, which you also weren't expecting, in an office environment similar to where you were attacked."

She nodded, relieved to hear how much sense the theory made. This wasn't a regression, just a different level of trigger than she'd faced before. It could be faced and dealt with, like anything else, now that it had been identified. "So as long as your biggest fantasy isn't making love on a desk, we should be okay."

"The only thing my fantasies include is you. The rest doesn't matter."

"Thanks. I know this is weird."

"Not really. From what I've been reading, it sounds pretty textbook."

"Wait, you've been reading up on PTSD?"

He nodded sheepishly. "I wanted to know what you were facing, so I could help."

She laughed, letting some of the tension bubble out with the sound. "More books, huh?"

"And articles on the internet. I'd actually like to go with you to your therapist sometime, if that would be okay. Not to intrude, or hear anything private. Just so maybe I could get some more tips on what I should and shouldn't do."

"Maybe. Let me think about it." She didn't like people even knowing she went to a therapist, let alone being part of the process. But Tyler was right. If it would help him understand, maybe it would be worth it.

Standing, she walked over to him and took his hand, waiting to see if there was a reaction. Nothing, just the normal flush of attraction she felt when they touched. Thank God. "Well, sir, some of us have work to do. But I'm glad you stopped by. Despite…well, everything."

He walked hand in hand with her to the doorway, then paused. "I'm glad I came, too. Call me tonight, okay? Let me know how you're doing."

"I will." Impulsively, she reached up on her toes to plant a quick peck of a kiss on his lips. No fear, no panic. Still, she didn't push it, happy to quit while she was ahead.

He smiled at the kiss and left, leaving her wanting more. It was a feeling she was becoming used to. But after a year of going through the motions, shutting off any emotion out of fear of losing control, it felt good to want, to feel so deeply. For Tyler, and for Kevin. At least with Tyler she felt they were moving in the right direction, no matter how slowly. With Kevin, she had a sinking fear that she'd made a wrong turn somewhere, and that if she didn't figure out her mistake soon, they would never find their way.

After seeing Dani, Tyler's next stop was the Paradise Animal Clinic. He was almost out of food for the kittens, and although he probably could have found something suitable at the grocery store he didn't want to switch if he didn't have to. And he needed to set up an appointment for their shots and checkups, anyway.

The clinic itself was back the way he had come, across the street from the bakery, and with the mild spring weather it was a pleasant walk. Soon enough the heat and humidity would make most of the natives take shelter in the air conditioning, but for now the sidewalks were full of residents like him going about their morning errands, as well as the occasional tourist. Several times he stopped to say hello to a friend or neighbor before reaching the low-slung building that housed the island's only veterinary hospital.

He took the landscaped path to the front door, noting the doggy-clean-up bag dispenser prominently displayed. Inside, several whimsical animal statues decorated the waiting room, and a television quietly played a loop of pet tips and health information. A woman clutching an irate-looking cat was seated on one of the cushioned benches, but otherwise the waiting area was empty. At the front desk a young woman in purple scrubs was refilling a treat jar with dog biscuits— probably a hot commodity in this place.

"Do you have people treats, too, or just the canine kind?"

She smiled and pointed to a candy dish on the other side of the counter. "Hard candy, no chocolate for safety reasons. Toxic to dogs, you know."

"That makes sense." He snagged a pineapple-shaped candy and pointed to one of the bags of food on the shelf behind her. "I'm going to need a bag of that kitten food, and I need to schedule an appointment for shots. Two of them. Kittens, I mean, not shots. I don't actually have any idea how many shots they need."

The woman—her name tag said Carly—laughed and handed him the bag of food. "Don't worry, we'll handle that part. How old are the kittens?"

"About nine weeks, I think? They actually came from here, so you might have it in your records. Dani Post picked them out for me."

"Oh, you're the one that got the kitties? How are they doing? I bet your daughters love them."

"The kittens are fine, and yes, the girls are crazy about them. I think they might love those cats more than they love me."

She smirked. "I'm sure that isn't true. After all, you're the one that let them get the kittens. That had to give you major bonus points."

"Good point. Maybe I'm safe for a little while."

"Probably." She typed something into the computer, and then made him an appointment for the following week for both kittens. He scheduled it for the afternoon so the girls could come, too, and then paid for the food. He was about to leave when he heard his name called.

"Tyler, how are you?"

Standing in the doorway to the back area of the clinic was Cassie, looking as if she'd just stepped out of the operating room.

"I'm good. Just setting up an appointment for the kittens, and getting them some food."

"Everything good with the cats? Adjusting well?"

"Definitely."

"And you and Dani, how is that going?"

He grinned. "Pretty well, I think. At least, it is when we get the time to see each other, which isn't as often as we'd like. We agree the kids come first, so between that and our jobs it's a little rough."

"Oh, yes. I remember those days well. Honestly, until I met Alex, I was convinced I'd be single forever. Or at least until Emma graduated and moved out. I just couldn't imagine finding the time or the energy for a relationship. But then I met Alex, and none of that really mattered. We made it work because walking away just wasn't an option."

He grinned, noting how her face lit up when she talked about her husband. "That's how I feel. Sure, it's not going to be easy, but I think Dani's worth it. Of course, I've had years to adjust to being a single father. She's just starting out as a parent, so it makes sense she's less sure of herself, and what she can handle."

"Well, if I know Dani, she can manage anything she sets her mind to."

"I agree."

She nodded and gestured toward the room behind her. "Well, I've got to get back to work, but it was good to see you. And if it means anything, I'm rooting for you. The whole town is."

"It does, thanks."

He left with a bit of a spring in his step. It wasn't just his own wishful thinking that made him believe they could make a go at things; Cassie thought so, too, and she knew the difficulties of dating while raising a child as much as anyone. Of course, they hadn't actually had a date, now that he thought about it. He'd have to see what they could work out, as far as child-free time. Maybe over the weekend. But until then, dinner together, even with the kids, would at least be a start. Somewhere nice, but not too fancy. He knew just the place.

Chapter Twelve

Dani waited in the car line with all the other parents as the teachers guided students to the appropriate vehicles. She'd gotten there early enough to be toward the head of the line, and before too long Kevin was climbing into the backseat, shoving his backpack onto the floor beside him.

"Did you have a good day?" she asked, watching him buckle up in the rearview mirror.

He shrugged and stared out the window.

"What did you do today?"

"I don't know. Stuff."

So much for small talk. Giving up, she turned her attention back to the road. Today, like most days, she took him back to the office with her for an hour or two so she could finish up her work. He generally did his homework while he waited, or chatted with her mom at the front desk. It wasn't a perfect system but it was working for now. She hadn't wanted to put him in after-care right away, and as long as she did another hour or so of work after he went to bed, she could keep on top of things.

At the office he kept up the silent treatment, stalking through the door ahead of her. Once inside, he went directly to the table and chairs in the waiting area and dug out his homework.

"Would you like a snack, Kevin?" her mother offered. "I've got some cookies and milk if you'd like."

"Yes, please. Thank you, Mrs. Post."

So whatever was keeping him from speaking to her didn't apply to her mother. Which meant whatever was bothering him was personal, something to do with her. And that hurt.

Heading back into her private office, she shut the door and fought the urge to cry. She was the grown-up; she had to keep it together. Breaking down wasn't an option. And tears wouldn't fix anything; they'd just mess up her makeup. No, what she needed was a plan. Or at least the start of one. Maybe there would be something useful in one of the parenting books Tyler had given her. She'd made it through part of one, but had plenty left to read. She'd start there, and if she couldn't come up with at least a glimmer of a solution she'd ask for help.

Kevin had his mentor meeting with Tyler tomorrow; maybe Tyler could get some information out of him. Whatever it was, knowing had to be better than wondering and worrying. If that didn't work, she'd call the social worker for advice. And she would make that appointment with the therapist that had been recommended. In fact she could do that right now. It was something she'd been meaning to get around to, but trying to figure out how to manage work, Tyler's school, the mentor program and everything else had made the thought of adding one more thing to their busy routine a bit intimidating. But obviously she needed to make the time, and soon.

Or not so soon, as it turned out. The therapist's secretary had been very polite, but unable to get them in for another three weeks. Phone calls to other therapists in the area had revealed similar wait times. So she went ahead and made the earliest appointment she could but said a silent prayer that they would be on better footing by the time it rolled around.

As soon as she hung up, her phone rang again. Checking the screen, she was relieved to see Tyler's name pop up. "Hey, I was just about to call you."

"Well, I beat you to it. What's up?"

"I'm worried about Kevin. He's still giving me the silent treatment, and I have no idea why. I tried to get an appointment with a therapist, but it's going to be weeks. The only person he seems to be on speaking terms with is my mom, but he barely knows her. I don't think he's likely to open up to her, not yet."

"I can try to talk to him, if you want."

Relief rushed through her. "I was hoping you'd say that. I hate asking—I feel like I should be able to handle this myself. I'm his parent now, for better or for worse. But…"

"But there is no shame in asking for help. Maybe he just needs a man-to-man chat. Sometimes guys like to talk to other guys. It could be as simple as that."

"I hope so. And Tyler, can you do me a favor?"

"Of course, what is it?"

"Don't tell him I told you about this. I don't want him to think we are ganging up on him." Even if they were.

"My lips are sealed. I'll just feel out how things are going in general—with school, you, et cetera. Nothing specific, I promise."

"Thanks. You're the best."

"About time you realized it," he quipped, lifting her spirits.

"Seriously, you are. I feel like I'm bringing all this drama into your life—"

"Life is drama. Crap happens. I'm sure in a few weeks I'll be the one with a problem, begging you to help me."

"Somehow I doubt that. Unless you get into some sort of legal dilemma. Then I'm your girl."

"You're my girl, no matter what. And speaking of that, I'd like to take you to dinner tomorrow night."

"Aww, that's sweet but I can't. I've got Kevin."

"I know. He's invited, too."

"Really?"

"Sure, I'll bring the girls, too. I know it's not the most romantic idea, but I'd rather spend time with you and the kids than without you. I was thinking we'd go out for pizza all together. I'll already have Kevin with me. You just have to meet me there. Say around six o'clock?"

"I can't wait." And she really couldn't. Lord, he'd been at her office having coffee with her just a matter of hours ago, and already she missed him. Heck, she'd been missing him from the moment he left.

They said their goodbyes, and Dani got back to

work, determined to trust that things would work out. But in the back of her mind, she couldn't help but wonder if she was being optimistic or naive.

Tyler rang up a customer's purchase while trying to keep an eye on Kevin. He'd asked the boy to sweep the floor as part of his attempt to earn his own bat. Normally Kevin did the job well, and without complaint. Today, however, he'd first argued the floor didn't need sweeping, then done such a lousy job Tyler had been forced to send him back to redo it. He didn't like being hard on the kid, but he also wasn't going to allow him to shirk his responsibilities. Kevin had agreed to the plan, and Tyler wanted to see that he stuck with it. Backing out of an agreement wasn't acceptable, not without a good reason. And so far, Kevin hadn't given him any reasons at all. In fact, he'd barely spoken. Nothing when Tyler had picked him up from school, nothing when they'd hung out in the break room having a snack and nothing since. Except, of course, to argue. Now he was back to being silent, and Tyler wasn't sure if that was better or worse than the bickering.

Bringing his attention back to the job at hand, he forced himself to smile. "Here you go, sir. The receipt is in the bag. Have a nice day."

"You, too."

Once the customer had left Tyler took a minute to check on the girls in the break room. They were both coloring quietly, so he just waved and went to look for Kevin. He found him standing in the middle of an aisle, leaning on the broom, staring off into space. He didn't look bored, though; he looked concerned. Scared, even. Dani was right: something was up.

"Hey, buddy. Listen, I wasn't trying to be mean before. I just know you're capable of doing a good job, as good as anyone. So that's what I expect. And I want you to earn that bat. You know that, right?"

He startled, and started shoving the broom half-heartedly across the floor. "Yeah, I guess."

"You guess?" He took the broom from the boy and crouched down so he could make eye contact. "Listen, I only want what's best for you. Dani, too. If we seem like we're messing up, you can tell us. I might not agree, but I'll listen."

"Can I have the broom back now, so I can finish?"

Tyler couldn't be sure, but he almost thought he'd caught a glimpse of tears in Kevin's eyes. Not wanting to make the boy cry, he handed back the broom. "Sure. But Kevin, if something's bothering you, you can tell me. I'll help you, no matter what it is." He waited for a response, but got nothing. "So…is there anything you want to talk about? Maybe something at school, or with Dani? It's got to be hard, adjusting to a new foster home."

"I just want to finish sweeping, okay?"

Sensing he'd get nowhere by pushing, Tyler nodded and walked away, giving him some space. He'd done his best; the rest was up to Kevin. Hopefully at least some of what he'd said got through to him, and after he had a chance to think about it he'd be willing to talk.

In the meantime, he had work to do himself. So, while Kevin slowly swept, Tyler restocked some of the low inventory. He'd planned to have Kevin mop as well, but given how late it was, he decided to cut the kid some slack and sent him to color or play in the break room for a few minutes while he finished up.

Normally he stayed open until six on a Tuesday, but no one was likely to mind if he hung the Closed sign out a few minutes early. He flipped it over and was about to lock the door when he spied Dani coming up the sidewalk. He let out a long, low whistle at her short skirt and high heels, and was rewarded with an embarrassed smile.

"I know you said to meet you at the restaurant, but I was running a few minutes early, and well… I couldn't wait."

"To see me, or to eat dinner?"

"Both." She glanced around at the empty room, then gave him a quick kiss on the lips. "But mostly to see you." She waited for him to lock the door, then lowered her voice. "Also, I was hoping you'd have some news about Kevin. Did you tell you anything?"

He shook his head, wishing he had better news. "He shut me out, same as you."

Her smile fell, and a worried crease marred her brow. "Well, crap. I really was hoping he'd confide in you."

Tyler brushed a loose hair off of her cheek, letting his fingers linger. "Hey, don't give up. I think he will, in time. And look at it this way—at least you know it's not just you."

A sad smile crossed her lips. "I suppose you're right." Drawing her shoulders back, she nodded to the break room. "Everyone ready? Because I'm thinking I need some carbs, and quick."

"That's the spirit." It was good to see her rallying, even if only on the surface. Once again, her strength came through. "Come on, kids, let's go! Pizza time!"

Adelaide and Amy came barreling out, dodging

him in favor of smothering Dani with hugs. Behind them trailed Kevin. Looking at the blank expression on the formerly exuberant boy's face nearly broke Tyler's heart. Somehow, they'd get Kevin smiling again.

Lou's Pizza was an institution in Paradise. It had been part of the downtown scene as long as anyone could remember. More important than its history, however, was its food. If you wanted old-style, handmade dough piled with the freshest toppings this side of Italy, Lou's was where you went. A favorite with everyone, from the tourist who just happened to wander in, to the seniors who had been eating there for decades, and everyone in between, especially the children of the island.

Straight-A report cards and T-ball losses were celebrated at Lou's. It was the kind of place you could relax and be yourself in. Dani's first date had been at the corner booth, an occasion more memorable for the large soda her date had spilled on her than for the boy himself. She had assumed that would be her worst memory of the place, but Kevin was working to prove her wrong.

"I'm hungry," he whined.

"I know. You've said it at least six times since we sat down." She stopped herself—griping back wasn't going to help. Calming herself, she tried again. "They don't make the pizzas until you order them, so it takes a little bit. The food will be here soon, I promise."

He frowned, and drummed his fingers on the table, waves of frustration pouring off of him.

Definitely an emotion she could relate to right now. Not that she was particularly hungry; Kevin's behavior was quickly eroding her appetite. Even the twins were eyeing him cautiously, as if unsure why the older boy they had looked up to was suddenly acting like he had never heard of good manners. But frustration, that she had in spades. It wasn't just his attitude that was becoming a real problem—more than that, being shut out over and over again was wearing on her patience. She'd give anything to help him; why couldn't he see that? Didn't he know how much she cared about him and his happiness?

Distracted, she barely noticed when their food arrived, other than it put an end to Kevin's demands. Instead, he switched to complaining that the cheese was too hot and the pepperoni was too spicy. Each negative remark tightened the knot in Dani's stomach. She had the eerie feeling that something was about to happen, something not good, and that feeling intensified as the meal dragged on. Twisting her napkin in her lap, she wracked her brain for a way to help. Tyler looked just as stymied by the situation, the muscles of his face taut, his brow furrowed. So much for a fun, maybe even romantic evening.

She was about to give in and call it a night when Tyler's parents walked in. At least, she recognized his mother from the night she'd brought the girls by. She just assumed the grey-haired man in jeans and a T-shirt with her was Tyler's father.

She pointed them out, and Tyler stood to greet them. "Hi, Mom. Hi, Dad. Mom, you remember Dani, and this is Kevin." He pointed out each one in turn. "We're just finishing up our dinner."

"That's wonderful. And it looks delicious." She

smiled at Kevin. "So, was yours good? Pepperoni pizza is my favorite, too."

"No. I hated it. This place sucks."

"Kevin!" Embarrassment and worry shredded the last bit of patience she'd had left. "What on earth is the matter with you?"

"Nothing." He scowled, his face turning as red as the sauce as everyone at the table turned to stare at him.

"Well, something is. I wish you'd just tell me what's wrong, so I could help you with it."

Kevin stood up abruptly, knocking over his pizza plate and spilling Adelaide's milk. A tear slipped down his freckled cheek as he surveyed the mess. "See what you made me do? Why can't you just leave me alone? You want to know what's wrong? Everyone bugging me all the time, wanting to know my business, that's what's wrong! I just want you to stop pestering me. And I want to quit the stupid mentor program. And," he choked out over a sob, "I want a new foster mom."

Stunned, Dani stood there as milk spread across the table, unable to comprehend what he was saying. He wanted to move out? "Kevin—"

"I said, leave me alone!" And then, before she could get another word in, he pushed past the girls and sprinted for the door. He was out of the restaurant and running down the street, and Adelaide was crying about her milk and half the room was staring at them all.

"I've got to stop him." She grabbed her purse and started to dig out her wallet.

Tyler pushed her toward the door. "I've got this. Just go."

"Thanks."

Leaving him and his wide-eyed parents standing there, she bolted for the door, dodging chairs and a waiter carrying a huge pizza tray. Outside, she turned to the left, the direction she'd seen him take through the plate glass windows. Downtown was still relatively busy, with families walking home from dinner, teens hanging out at the ice-cream parlor and an assortment of frazzled shoppers running errands after a day of work. It would be easy for a small boy to blend in, hiding amongst the pedestrians. Or he could have ducked into any of the open stores, knowing that she'd be right behind him.

Pulling up a picture of him on her phone to show to the shopkeepers, she bit her lip not to cry. She didn't have time to break down; Kevin needed her. And she wasn't going to let him down.

Chapter Thirteen

Tyler grabbed a handful of napkins and started mopping up the table while trying to soothe Adelaide. Who knew people actually did cry over spilled milk? "The waiter will get you another one."

"But what about Kevin?" she asked between sobs.

"Yeah, he just left. Without a grown-up," Amy said in awe.

"Dani will find him, don't worry." At least, he hoped she would. Paradise wasn't a big island but there were still plenty of places to hide if you were a boy as small as Kevin.

"Tyler, honey, why don't you help her? We can handle the girls." His mother took the napkins from him and wiped at Adelaide's damp shirt.

"Are you sure?" He didn't want to upset the twins any further, but if Dani was going to find Kevin, an extra body could make all the difference.

"Absolutely." His father sat down next to Amy, his stance making it clear he wasn't going to take no for an answer. "We'll let them finish their meal, and then we can take them back to your house and get them ready for bed. We'll wait there for you. Take as long as you need."

"Thanks, guys. I appreciate it. I'll let you know when we find him."

His father nodded brusquely, and Tyler felt a swell of gratitude. He and his father had been through some rough patches, but they had reached a point where at the end of the day he knew both his parents were there for him when he needed them. That kind of support made such a difference in who he was, and it was something Kevin had never really known. All the more reason to find him and get to the bottom of this nonsense. He didn't believe for one minute that Kevin really wanted to be left alone. No child did. But something was making him feel he had to push away everyone that cared about him, and Tyler wasn't going to rest until he found out why.

Whatever it was, it had to have happened recently. He'd been fine last week, and had seemed to really enjoy camping on Saturday. Sunday had been the start of the sullen attitude, the changed behavior. But what could have happened to cause such a switch, literally overnight? Was it something one of them had said? He wracked his brain, but couldn't think of anything that could have been taken badly.

Maybe it wasn't something they'd said to him, but something they'd done? Both he and Dani, by unspoken agreement, limited any public displays of affection in front of the kids, but there had been a few times he'd held her hand, or given her a quick hug. Kevin was a perceptive kid; he may have realized there was more than friendship between the two adults in his life. Maybe it was that simple—he didn't want to share Dani.

If so, he hoped they would talk it over, and work something out. The last thing Tyler wanted was to lose Dani when they were finally on the same page, but if that was what it took, he'd have to. Kevin's needs had to come before his own. But just the thought of letting her go made him break into a cold sweat.

Taking the same direction Dani had, he immediately realized the magnitude of the problem. There were too many stores still open, and too many side streets to turn onto. He could be anywhere by now. Setting off on foot, he briefly scanned the front windows of each business he passed. Several were tourist-type shops, where a small boy would stick out. A nail salon wasn't a likely hiding spot, either. Across the street was the ice-cream parlor where they'd ended up on their first mentor visit. That was more promising. Enough other kids for him to easily blend in, and if he had any of his allowance on him he could drown his sorrows in a sundae.

Dodging cars, he crossed against the light and swung the door open. All the tables, inside and out, were packed, with more people gathered at the glass display case. But none of them was Kevin. Disappointed, he headed back to the street and nearly ran into Dani. He'd been so focused on looking for a child he hadn't even noticed her. She had her phone out, showing Kevin's picture to the teenagers outside. A smart idea, one he should have thought of.

She looked up when he tapped her on the shoulder, her face tight with grief. "Kevin?"

He shook his head, hating to disappoint her.

Her jaw clenched, but other than that she gave no reaction, just nodded. "Then we'll just keep looking."

Dani started for the next business, Tyler at her side. Logically, splitting up would make more sense. They could cover twice as much ground that way. But now that he was with her she wasn't sure she could do this on her own. Every bit of her strength right now was channeled into staying positive, into being productive. But even as she politely asked strangers if they recognized his picture the voice in her head was questioning everything that had led up to this point. Including agreeing to foster him at all.

Her intentions had been good, but was that enough? She didn't have any experience with children, other than the few times she'd babysat her young nephew. And he wasn't even a year old yet. She didn't know a thing about preadolescent boys, or kids who had been through trauma like Kevin had. Really, it was audacious that she'd ever even considered the idea. He should have gone to someone with more experience, someone older. Someone who could have offered him more.

But even as she thought that, her heart rebelled. She might not have the experience or even the wisdom of other foster parents, but she had as much love as any of them. And she did love Kevin. More than she'd known was possible, especially in such a short time. Maybe that was just the way her heart worked, as an on or off switch, rather than in shades of gray. Because as much as she'd come to love Kevin, she'd also fallen for the man at her side, the one that had stood up to her when she'd railed at him on Kevin's behalf. Who'd pushed her to consider all the angles before fostering Kevin. And who had been there, supporting her ever since.

In a way, she'd fallen for both of them at the same time. And yet, she'd never told either of them. Maybe if Kevin had known how she felt, he wouldn't have run off.

Or would that have made it worse? Maybe it was the opposite problem; maybe she'd come on too strong. She had been trying so hard; maybe all that effort had seemed overwhelming to him. Smothering even. Hadn't he said that he just wanted to be left alone? Obviously she couldn't leave him totally alone, but maybe she could have been a bit more hands-off, let him be a bit more independent.

That didn't feel right, but obviously her instincts couldn't be trusted. And it made sense, on a logical level. Lots of people preferred to ease into relationships. Look at her own reaction to Tyler. He'd been interested in her from the start, but she'd pushed him away, over and over again. And then, when she finally agreed to give things a try, she'd been half-hearted about it, telling him she wanted to take it day by day. To just see what happened. A lukewarm response if ever there was one. And not because she wasn't interested, but because she was scared. Scared she'd fall hard and end up hurt.

Now that rang true. She could feel it in her bones. Kevin wasn't just angry. He was scared. She knew a lot about fear. The difference was, she was an adult. She could use her experience and reason to overcome that fear. And some pretty intense therapy hadn't hurt, either. Now, looking over at the man who had stolen her heart, it was hard to believe that she'd tried to keep him at arm's length. That she had ever pushed him away. But that breakthrough had taken time, and a lot of communication.

Maybe she could help Kevin with that. Let him know about her own fears, and how she had overcome them. Help him to see that risking his heart was better than hiding it away. Of course, she hadn't faced all of her demons yet. She'd been working on it, looking in to what, if anything, she could do about what had happened to her in Jacksonville. Until tonight she had avoided taking the next step, but maybe if she could convince Kevin to be brave, it would be a sign that it was time for her to find her own courage.

But first, she had to find him. Reaching out for Tyler, she found comfort and strength in his hand as it held hers. "I just wish we knew where he might go, instead of wandering aimlessly like this. I mean, there must be somewhere he feels safe, right?"

Tyler stopped, pulling her to a standstill. "You know…you may be on to something. I know when I was a kid his age the ballpark was my second home. I spent more hours there than I did my own house. Think he might go there?"

The park made as much sense as anywhere. He'd been in and out of different homes, but that would have been a constant in his life. Somewhere he felt connected to. Sadly, her own home didn't fit that bill. Not yet. It was something she'd address as soon as she found him. She'd do whatever it took to convince him to stay, to give her another chance.

And then, when things with Kevin were settled, she'd tell Tyler how she felt. Both of the men in her life deserved to know she loved them.

Tyler matched his stride to Dani's, both anxious to see if his hunch was right. The park wasn't far, but the whole way there he kept wondering if all of this was his fault. If he'd stayed away from Dani, would Kevin have gotten more attention, felt safer? Had he been interfering with their relationship, despite his pledge not to? And what about the initial arrest—would they all have been better off if he hadn't pressed charges? Having probation hanging over him had to be stressful to a boy Kevin's age. And he wasn't a bad kid. He'd just made a stupid decision. Maybe he should have just let him go with a warning.

Of course, then he never would have met Dani. And whatever was going on with Kevin, he couldn't find a way to regret her coming into his life. She'd drawn him out, reminded him what living was all about. He'd spent the last few years moving through his life, one step at a time, as if in a dream. Then she'd come along, and he'd finally come truly awake for the first time since his wife died. He didn't like admitting that. His daughters should have been enough to keep him going. And in almost every way that mattered, they were. But something in his soul had died when he'd buried his wife, and it had been reborn when he met Dani.

She was his second chance at life, not just love. And as selfish as it was, he didn't want to let that go. Gripping her hand, he forced himself to stay calm. Until they found Kevin, his own feelings would have to go on the back burner. Afterward, well, he'd deal with that when the time came.

"Do you think we should call the police?" Dani's question jarred him out of his head and back to the matter at hand.

"No. Not yet. Let's see if he's at the park first." He said a silent prayer that waiting was the right answer. If Kevin wasn't there, would they regret not calling in the police sooner? And if the police did end up being involved, how would that look to social services? Dani's competency as a foster parent could be questioned. That, coupled with Kevin's recent determination to leave, could mean she'd lose custody of the boy. She'd be devastated.

As hard as it had been for her to leap into parenting so quickly, there was no doubt in his mind that she loved the boy. No one could be a better parent than she would be to him, but depending on how the night turned out she might not have a choice in the matter. Nor would Kevin, and despite what he had said, Tyler didn't think the boy really wanted that.

The entrance to the park was well lit, but fairly empty. Walking under the large stone arch was like walking into another world. Gone were the houses and businesses, which were replaced by trees that cast ominous shadows onto the path. Beside him Dani shivered.

"Are you cold?" Spring in Florida tended to be warm, but there was a cool breeze tonight. Another reason to find Kevin quickly—he'd been dressed in shorts and a T-shirt.

"No. Just kind of creeped out," she admitted sheepishly. "This place looks a lot different in the daylight."

"Agreed. But they'll be more people, and lights, over by the ball fields. Little League games run until eight."

She nodded and picked up the pace. They passed the playground where he'd first met her, empty now except for a stuffed toy someone had forgotten. Beyond that the path curved, and they emerged into a brightly lit area with basketball and racquetball courts. Here there were plenty of people, adults mostly, catching up with friends and getting in some exercise. Straight ahead were the baseball fields.

Each step tightened the tension in his shoulders, and despite the weather he felt a trickle of sweat drip down his back. The path circled the field, taking them by the concession stand, where kids of all ages congregated, bonding over hot dogs and snow cones. Beyond that were the stands, metal bleachers that shone in the bright overhead lights. At first, it looked like a dead end. But there, in the very top row, was a small boy with brown hair, hunched down as if the weight of the world was resting on his small shoulders.

"Kevin!" Dani's shout rang in his ears as she ran up the bleachers. Following behind her, he said a silent prayer of thanks. Whatever happened now, at least they knew he was safe, if a little the worse for wear. He looked like he'd been crying; his eyes were bloodshot and his cheeks tearstained. And if the look on Dani's face was any indication, his night wasn't about to get any easier.

"Kevin McCarthy, what on earth were you thinking? You had us all worried sick! We were getting ready to call the cops, we were so scared!"

Kevin's eyes widened in shock. "You were going to call the police? Are they coming? Are they going to take me to jail because I messed up while I was on probation?" Fear blanched his face, making his freckles stand out in sharp relief. "Please, Dani, don't make me go to jail. I'm sorry I ran away. Really, I am."

Dani's heart ripped in two at the little boy's words. What was she doing, yelling at the poor child? He was obviously scared and here she was, making it worse. No wonder he'd wanted to run away from her. Taking a deep breath, she started over. "Nobody is sending you to jail. We were just scared, that's all." Sitting down next to him, she took in his tear-spattered face, and wanted to scoop him up onto her lap. Instead, she asked, "Are you okay?"

He nodded hesitantly. "I'm sorry I upset you."

"Yeah, well, sometimes that happens. But it doesn't mean you're going to jail, or anywhere else other than back to my place. At least for tonight. I know you said you want to go live somewhere else, but I'm warning you, I'm going to try to change your mind. I love you, and I want you to stay with me. So I'm hoping that whatever it is that has you so upset, we can work on it and figure it out together. What do you think?"

Kevin blinked, his dark eyelashes fanning up and down in surprise. "You...love me?"

"You bet I do."

Without warning he threw himself at her, hugging her so hard she had to fight to breathe. But she wasn't going to complain. Wrapping her arms around him, she squeezed back, and waited for him to let go. When he finally did, she had to ask. "I take it that means you don't want to move out?"

He shook his head.

"Then why on earth did you say all those things?"

"Because I wanted you and Tyler to be happy together."

Confused, she tried to make sense of that, and failed. "I don't understand. Why did you think acting this way, and saying you don't want to live with me, would make us happy?"

"Because when we were camping, I heard you say you want to be with him, but you had to put me first. What if something happens, and you don't have time for both of us? If you're my foster mother, you would have to pick me. That would make you sad, and I don't want you to be sad."

Dani's jaw dropped at his admission. That's what he'd been thinking?

Eyes earnestly seeking hers, he continued, "And if you guys stay together, you might get married. Then Amy and Adelaide would have a mother and a father. I've never had two parents, so I'm used to it, but they aren't. They miss having a mom—they told me so. And they are good kids, not like me. They deserve two parents. So I figured I'd just be bad, and you'd give me back. Then you and Tyler could be together, and they'd get a mom, and everyone would be happy."

Dani swallowed back the tears that clogged her throat. "First of all, I would definitely not be happy if you didn't want to live with me anymore. So that won't work. And second of all, what do you mean, they're good and you're not?" Where on earth had he gotten that idea?

"Because I tried to steal something," he explained,

as if it was totally obvious. "I got arrested. I'm on probation. That means I'm a bad kid."

Now there was no holding back her tears. So she let them flow as she gripped his shoulders, getting eye-to-eye with him, making sure he heard every word she was about to say. "Don't you ever say that again. You are not a bad kid. You just made a mistake. We all make mistakes. That doesn't change who you are inside. And you, Kevin McCarthy, are a terrific kid, inside and out."

"But—"

"No buts. That's the truth. The only important thing is that you face your mistakes and learn from them. And you did that. You sat in that courtroom, and you took your sentence, and you've been working hard to do what the judge said to do. You're making it right, and that's what counts."

He turned to Tyler, as if needing confirmation. "Is that true?"

He smiled warmly, his eyes harboring affection and a bit of humor. "That everyone makes mistakes? I'm afraid so. And you keep making them, even when you're all grown up. But like Dani said, when it happens you just need to admit it and learn from it. The only thing to be ashamed of is if you ignore them, or deny them. Because then those mistakes will follow you, and never really let you go."

Dani listened, and thought of her own past. It had been a mistake for her to leave Jacksonville without pressing charges, or at least confronting her superiors about what had been going on. Maybe she just hadn't been ready, but either way, ignoring that decision had indeed cost her. Just like Tyler had said, it followed her, interfering with her present. If she wanted to move forward, she was going to need to deal with the mess she'd left. And now she had a feeling she was strong enough to do it.

"So, kiddo, are you ready to come back home?"

"Well, what about you and Tyler?"

She looked at Tyler and then back at Kevin, a feeling of peace settling over her. "Don't you worry about Tyler and me. We're grown-ups and can handle our own affairs, thank you very much. You just promise me you won't run off again, and that if you are worried about something, you'll talk to someone about it. Okay?"

"Okay."

He stood up, and started down the steps with them, one on either side. They walked that way all the way back to where Dani's car was, near her office. She made sure he was buckled in, then gave Tyler a quick hug and a peck on the cheek, mindful of Kevin watching them through the car window.

"Glad we found him, and that everything is going to be okay. I can't believe he had all that going on inside that head of his." Tyler shook his own in disbelief. "Amazing what kids come up with."

"Seriously. Anyway, I'll be in touch. Might be a day or two—I'm going to be busy for a bit." Not wanting him to ask any questions, she opened her car door and got in. "Oh, and thanks again for helping tonight. I was really glad to have you with me."

He looked puzzled, but just nodded and waved as she drove off.

Maybe it was cowardly of her to leave things that way, especially after everything they had been through, but what she was going to be dealing with, she needed to face alone. If all went well, she'd share everything with him when she got back. Because in the morning she was going to Jacksonville.

Chapter Fourteen

It had been less than forty-eight hours since Tyler had last seen Dani, the night they found Kevin. In the grand scheme of things, a very short time. But that was still way too long. She'd said she was going to be busy, and he'd accepted that. She had her job, and she and Kevin had a lot to talk about. Fine. But he hadn't expected total radio silence. No phone calls, no texts, nothing.

More than once he'd started to call her, then stopped before hitting the green button. He didn't want to push her, not when things were going so well. Making her feel claustrophobic wasn't a good strategy. And yet here he was, standing in front of her office with a bouquet of flowers and a steaming cup of coffee. She'd appreciated him stopping by once before; hopefully it would go as well today. Besides, what woman didn't like flowers? And it had pained him to realize that, just as they had never had a proper date, he'd never given her flowers. Definitely time to remedy that oversight.

Entering the cool, dim office space, he immediately spied Dani's mother. She waved hello, then motioned to the phone at her ear. No problem; he could find her office himself. Waving back, he knocked quickly on Dani's door and then swung it open, holding the flowers out in front of him as an offering.

To an empty room.

The lights were off, the computer was off and it didn't look like anyone was around. Strange. It was two o'clock in the afternoon; he had expected her to be working. Kevin's school didn't get out for another hour and a half, so she wouldn't be there.

"She's gone."

Tyler spun around to find Dani's mother in the doorway, her eyes dark with sympathy. "She left yesterday. I'm sorry, I thought you knew."

He looked down at the flowers in his hands. "No. I didn't know. Where is she?" Maybe she'd had a work trip to attend to? A family emergency? He waited, praying for some kind of logical explanation, and yet knowing deep down he wasn't going to get one.

She shrugged. "I don't know. She came in yesterday as normal, locked herself in her office for about an hour or so, then came out and said she needed to take a few days off. She said it was a personal matter, and I didn't want to pry." She smiled sadly. "To tell the truth, I thought maybe she was having a romantic rendezvous with you and just didn't want to admit it to her old-fashioned mom." She glanced at the bouquet, then back at him. "I guess not."

"Definitely not." Where on earth could she have

gone? Then he paused, thinking of something. "What about Kevin? Did she take him with her? Or did he—"

"He's with the Cunninghams, just until Dani gets back," she assured him. "He's helping them pack and get ready for their move. The Cunninghams were thrilled to have him, and he was excited to see them again. As young as he is, I think he'll be a big help. Moving is hard, especially on the elderly."

Tyler nodded, glad at least that Tyler hadn't changed his mind again about wanting to live with Dani. For a brief moment he'd been afraid that Dani had taken off because Kevin had rejected her. But if that had been the case, she would have called him.

None of this made any sense. "Do you know when she's coming back?" If she was coming back.

"She should be back sometime tomorrow evening. That's all I know." She turned, and then stopped. "Would you like me to put the flowers in water? I could leave them on her desk for when she gets back."

"Um, sure. Thank you." He handed them over, his head still spinning. "Want some coffee, too? Cream and sugar?"

"I'm more of a tea drinker, sorry. Besides, I have a feeling maybe you need it yourself."

"Good point." Maybe the hit of caffeine would help him make sense of Dani's disappearing. "If you hear from her, will you tell her I stopped by?"

"Of course. And Tyler, I'm sure it has nothing to do with you. She cares about you, I can tell."

"Thanks. I appreciate that." Even if he wasn't ready to believe it. He didn't want to believe the worst, but she'd always said that Kevin would come first, that if there was a conflict she'd choose him. And there had been plenty of conflict lately. Tyler thought they had worked it all out, that Kevin was okay with them being together. But maybe he'd read too much into everything. Emotions had been high, and he'd been so relieved to find the boy safe that maybe he'd misunderstood.

Or maybe Kevin was okay with the idea, but Dani wasn't. She could have decided the other night was a sign, showing that she couldn't handle everything. Which wasn't true; he knew she was strong enough to tackle the world if she wanted to. But maybe she had doubts. He racked his brain, trying to remember what she'd said two nights ago, what words she'd used.

The only thing he could recall was when she'd told Kevin that they were adults, and would work it out. At the time he'd assumed that meant they would figure out a way to be together and make everyone involved happy. But now that she'd left without a word of good-bye, he had to think she meant something else. Had she left town to give herself the space to figure out a way to break up with him? Or was he supposed to just forget about her? Out of sight, out of mind?

No way was that going to happen. She could be on the other side of the globe and he wouldn't forget about her, wouldn't stop thinking about her. Not for one minute. He loved her, and the minute he found her, he was going to tell her so.

Dani stood in the Jacksonville Police Department, her purse held tightly in both hands, mainly to keep them from shaking. She'd spent the past day and a half in a mad scramble planning for this moment, and now that it was here she just wanted to run back to her car and head for home. She wouldn't do that, though. She'd come too far. And she'd reached the point where making her future meant facing the past.

"Ma'am, can you step this way, please?" A young officer who looked like he should be sitting in a high school classroom, not wearing a badge, escorted her down a sterile hallway to a private room, containing a small table, four hardback chairs and a video camera.

Was this an interrogation room? She wasn't a suspect; she was here to file a report. She was about to tell him as much when a woman, also in uniform, approached. "Hi, Ms. Post? I'm Officer Stokes. I'll be taking your statement." She nodded to the chairs. "I apologize for the accommodations, but given the nature of the complaint I thought you'd prefer some privacy. If you'd rather we do this at my desk, we can, but it's a bit of a madhouse upstairs."

"No, this is fine." A bit creepy, but she was right. Privacy was better. It was going to be hard enough to talk about this without an audience.

Taking a seat, she placed her purse on the table and hugged her arms into her body. Officer Stokes sat across from her and smiled warmly. "Before we start, would you like some coffee, or a soda, or anything? I can have someone bring something in. It's no trouble."

"No, thank you. I've had enough caffeine over the last two days to last me a lifetime."

She chuckled. "I know what that's like. But if you change your mind just let me know. And if you need a break, that's fine, too. We're not in any rush. If at any point you say stop, we'll stop, and we won't start again until you're ready."

Dani soon realized that "no rush" wasn't an exaggeration. The process of giving her statement, recorded on video, took hours. Not because she had that much to say, but because she was asked to go over and over it, clarifying various points, each time starting over from the beginning. Twice she had to take a break, just to get out of that room for a minute. She used the restroom, splashed water on her face and fixed her lipstick. Anything to delay going back in there and repeating it all again.

Finally, though, that portion of the process was over. Next she was asked why she'd waited so long to report what happened. She'd expected that question, but it still rankled.

"Because I didn't think anyone would believe me." At the time she'd been convinced that her own testimony wouldn't be enough. Realistically, it probably wouldn't. Which was why she'd spent yesterday making sure she had more than that.

"So why now? What changed?"

"Two things. First, I finally realized I needed to do something, or I'd never get past what happened. My therapist, and some other people in my life, helped me with that. And second, I now know I wasn't the only one he assaulted."

Officer Stokes raised one eyebrow, but otherwise controlled any reaction she might have had to that news. "And you know this how?"

"I tracked down any former female employees I could find. Some left because they got better offers elsewhere, or because they moved away. But five of them admitted to me that they quit because of sexual harassment. Four of them are still in the area. I have signed, notarized statements from them here." She pulled a thick envelope from her purse and slid it across the table. "They have all agreed to speak to you, including the woman who now lives in Miami. She said she'd be happy to drive up here, whatever it takes." All the women had expressed a sense of weird relief at finding out they were not the only victims. Some, like her, had sought out some therapy or other support. One was fighting depression and had said that knowing he might be put behind bars was better than any antidepressant in the world.

Hearing that had made her wish she'd acted months ago, when, after her therapist had encouraged her to find a productive way to channel her feelings she'd put some feelers out, using the internet and social media. She hadn't been ready to act on the information back then, but at least now justice was being done.

Officer Stokes read each page silently, then went to the doorway and called down the hall to someone. The same young man from earlier appeared a few seconds later. "Gary, can you go scan these pages for me? Thanks." He disappeared with the envelope and she resumed her place at the table.

"I'm not going to lie. As much as I believe your story, it's going to help a lot to have other women to corroborate a pattern of behavior. But I need you to tell me, on the record, how you found these women, and what you spoke of when you talked to them."

So she did. By the time she was done with the whole process and walking back out to her car, the sun was setting. She'd missed dinner, and she'd been too nervous to eat lunch earlier. On the way to her hotel she went through a drive-through and ordered what had to be a million calories of artery-clogging food, then took it back to her room. She probably would have been better off eating something healthy in the restaurant downstairs, but she'd had enough of people for one day. Instead, she changed into a ratty nightshirt, turned on an old movie and ate in bed. By the time the movie ended, she was more than ready to pass out.

She'd done it, though. As emotionally exhausted as she was, it had been worth it. The minute she'd left the police station, she'd felt as if a huge weight had been lifted off her shoulders. She still had to go back tomorrow, just to sign a written statement that Officer Stokes would be writing up. And if it did go to trial, she'd have to testify. But she'd deal with that if and when it happened. All she wanted now was to get a good night's sleep, and then to get out of this town and go home.

The drive home the next day seemed to drag on forever. From Jacksonville to the Palmetto County line, it was a straight shot down I-95, and then from there a rural highway connected her to the island. Normally it just took a few hours, but she'd hit rush hour coming out of the city and was way behind schedule. More traffic near Daytona, this time vacationers who were driving too slow, searching for their exit. By the time she hit her exit and the empty back roads, her nerves were shot and she had a decent headache brewing.

Of course, that couldn't all be blamed on the road conditions. It was also the loss of adrenaline, after running on fumes for three days straight. After she'd gotten home with Kevin the other night, she'd stayed up until the wee hours, emailing all the women she would need statements from before typing up her own story for the police.

Then in the morning she'd had to explain to Kevin what was going on, in words he could understand.

She'd told him that somebody had touched her in ways that he shouldn't, without her permission. That she'd been too scared to tell anyone when it happened, but after talking with him about how important it was to face things, she was feeling braver. That she was going to tell the police about the man, and there were other women he had been mean to as well. That if she didn't tell, he might keep doing it to other people.

Kevin had understood and had told her he was proud of her. She'd nearly lost it right then, but instead had hugged him and asked if he'd mind staying with the Cunninghams while she went to deal with things. He'd happily agreed. Once he was at school she'd spent the next few hours confirming times with the women she needed statements from, making hotel reservations, clearing her work schedule for a few days and making arrangements for Kevin. Thankfully the social worker had no issue with the Cunninghams' babysitting, and they were thrilled to have him back for a few days. They missed him, and promised to keep him busy as long as she wanted.

She almost told her mom what she was doing, but in the end had decided she'd rather explain after the fact. If she had to tell the story too many times before going to the police, she might chicken out before she got there. Thankfully her mother hadn't pressed her, and she'd been able to leave town with no one the wiser. Cowardly? Maybe. But she'd done what she had to do.

Tyler was a whole different issue. He already knew what had happened, and she knew, without a doubt, he would have supported her. But he would have wanted to go with her, and she needed to do this on her own: to prove to herself she could. And he might have wanted her to wait, to think it through, maybe talk to her therapist about it. All good advice, but she'd waited long enough. Too long, and she hadn't wanted to wait even one more day. She'd thought about calling him last night, but she wanted to tell him in person. But now that it was over she couldn't wait to see him. They could celebrate together.

Finally, just as the sun was starting to set, she drove over the arched bridge connecting Paradise Isle to the mainland. It was a drive she'd made probably a hundred times, but now more than ever she appreciated the understated beauty of the green island surrounded by turquoise waters. When she'd first come home, she'd been looking to hide and Paradise had been her safety net. Now, though, she was actively choosing to return, rather than feeling like it was the only place she had to go. Just three days in Jacksonville had been long enough to realize that the vibrant city wasn't what she wanted any longer. Maybe it never had been.

Ignoring the desire to drive straight to Tyler's place, she instead took a side road into the old neighborhood where her childhood home was located. She owed her parents the truth, and even if she didn't she wouldn't feel the entire incident was over if she was still hiding it from them. And sooner or later they were going to want to know where she had been. Might as well be now.

As expected, both her parents were home for the dinner hour, but her sister's car was also in the drive. That was a surprise—she hadn't even known Mollie was in town. She traveled back and forth with her husband between their home here in Paradise and an apartment in Atlanta, where they both had contacts in the art world. Having her here was a lucky break; it meant she wouldn't have to explain it all over again later.

She knocked quickly and then just let herself in. No matter how old she got, her mother insisted it was still her home and she didn't need to stand on ceremony. She found her mom finishing up dinner in the kitchen, some kind of skillet chicken, while her father and sister were setting out plates.

"Dani! You're back—are you staying for supper?" Her mother stopped stirring long enough to give her a quick hug.

"I can't. I've still got to go pick up Kevin. But thanks." She opened the fridge and found a pitcher of iced tea, just like always, and poured herself a glass. "I'll just have a cold drink."

"Whatever you want, honey. I'll have this finished in a minute, and it can sit in the oven and keep warm while we visit."

Her father looked up in alarm, causing Mollie to snicker.

"That's not necessary. I don't mind if you eat in front of me. And I think Dad's hungry."

Her father shot her a thumbs-up and quickly set the table, leaving the women in the kitchen.

"So," Mollie asked, waggling her eyebrows suggestively, "where were you? Romantic getaway?"

"Afraid not. Sorry to disappoint." She hip-checked her sister. "But don't worry, I'll explain everything."

And she did. Sitting there around the dining room table, where they had discussed so many other things, she told her family about her time in Jacksonville, why she had left and why she had returned this week. And just like they always had, they supported her.

Her mother, with tears in her eyes, had simply said she was glad Dani was okay, and happy she'd felt comfortable telling them the truth. Mollie had muttered a few unladylike words under her breath at key points in the story, then given her a hug. And her dad…he'd sat in stone-faced silence, demonstrating the control he was known for in both the courtroom and in his personal life. The only clue to his feelings had been a vein throbbing at his temple. At the end of her tale he had told her, with a voice gruff with emotion, that he was proud of her. And that he'd be sure never to refer any business to that law firm again. Then he'd excused himself, his food untouched, and gone for a walk.

Her heart hurt for him. She rose, pushing back her chair to go after him, when her mother stopped her with a hand on her arm. "Let him go. He'll be fine. He just doesn't like the thought of anyone hurting his baby girl. But if you were strong enough to handle all this, he is, too. He just needs some time to process it."

She nodded. She'd had a year to learn to live with what had happened—they were hearing it for the first time. They'd all need a bit of time to process. But that was okay. She was learning that sometimes, things just took time.

And other things, well, they happened fast, and there was no reason to fight that, either.

Tyler checked the clock and resisted the urge to throw the dirty plate he was washing. It had only been five minutes since he'd last looked. At this rate he wouldn't make it through the night with his sanity intact. Dani's mom had said she was expected home this evening. Well, it was past seven at night. Surely she was back by now.

Unless she wasn't coming back. That thought, ridiculous as it was, refused to be totally vanquished. The woman had a life here. She had a job, her family and Kevin. She had him, damn it. She had to come back.

But she had up and left once before, when things got crazy. But that was different. She'd been backed into a corner then, with no support. Paradise, with all its flaws, was nothing if not full of people who cared for each other. And she had no reason to run. He'd been careful not to push her too hard, and things had worked out with Kevin. So she'd be back. At least that was the mantra he had been repeating over and over as he cleaned up the kitchen after dinner.

He continued to do so as he bathed the girls, read them a story and tucked them in. But as the clock inched past eight he found himself wondering if he was just deluding himself. Three days with no contact wasn't exactly a promising sign for their relationship. And sitting here, feeling sorry for himself, wasn't helping. Maybe a run would calm his thoughts and keep him busy until he found out what she was doing and where he stood.

With that thought in mind, he called his mom. She lived only a few blocks away and as a true night owl she never minded popping over to keep an eye on the girls as they slept. Sure enough, she said she'd be right over.

He changed into shorts and a pair of running shoes

while waiting, being careful not to wake the girls. When his mother knocked on the door five minutes later, her knitting bag in hand, he was ready to go. "I'll be back in an hour. Call me if they wake up or you need anything."

She patted her bag. "Between this and reruns on TV, I'll be fine. Have a good run."

"Thanks, Mom."

He took it slowly for the first quarter mile, and then turned on some speed, trying to outrun the fear that had haunted him since Dani left. Normally the rhythmic sound of his feet on pavement and the pounding of his own heart would be enough to drown out any of the worries on his mind. But not tonight. He couldn't outrun his feelings, no matter how fast or far he went. Finally, out of breath and nearly out of hope, he stopped. Bent over, hands on his knees, he fought back the anger mounting inside him. Fear had a way of doing that, twisting itself into anger or even hate.

He didn't hate Dani, of course. He couldn't. But he wasn't happy with her, and if anything the run had made it worse. Maybe she didn't want to be with him. That was her prerogative. But that didn't give her the right to treat him like a pair of shoes she'd gotten tired of, tossed in the trash and forgotten. He had feelings, and he deserved the decency of a proper goodbye, if nothing else. Something he planned to tell her, if he could ever freaking get a hold of her.

His phone vibrated in his pocket, and he grabbed it without looking, concerned something had happened back home. "Hello?"

"Hey. It's me, Dani. I was wondering if you could come over. I need to talk to you."

He glanced at his watch. He'd used up over half the hour he'd told his mom, but if he asked she'd stay longer. "Sure. I have some things to say to you, too." Plenty of them. Starting with "Where the hell were you?" and "Why haven't you returned my calls?" Maybe ending with some variation of "Would you mind telling me what's going on between us, because my heart can't take the suspense anymore?" Give or take, anyway.

Jogging back to the house, he stuck his head in and explained the situation to his mom, who, as anticipated, had no problem staying a bit longer. He debated taking a quick shower, or at least changing, but he was too anxious to hear what Dani had to say for herself to bother. If she didn't like him sweaty, well, she should have kept in touch better or called sooner.

The car ride only took a few minutes, not nearly enough time for his temper to fade. He knocked loudly and impatiently, and then felt a sliver of guilt, realizing Kevin, if he was even there, was probably sleeping. As upset as he was with Dani, he didn't want to disturb the boy.

She opened the door with a smile on her face, as if she hadn't been dodging his calls and avoiding him. Well, if she thought he was going to just pretend it hadn't happened, she had another think coming. He'd been supportive, and concerned and an all-around good guy since the day they met. But that didn't mean he was a pushover. It didn't mean she could treat him like dirt and just expect him to thank her for it. And he was going to tell her so, just as soon as she finished kissing him.

* * *

Dani hadn't planned on such a passionate greeting, but seeing Tyler, muscles bulging under his tank top, standing on her door like some kind of calendar pinup come to life, she hadn't been able to help herself. And for the record, she had no regrets about that decision. Being in his arms again felt like heaven after a long and grueling trip. Every inch of her reveled in the feel of his hard body against hers as she kissed him with all the pent-up longing and excitement she'd been holding back.

They hit the door hard, pushing it shut with their bodies as she dug her hands under the flimsy tank to find more skin. He increased his attack on her mouth in response, pulling her hips more firmly against his, making it obvious that he was as happy to see her, as she was to see him. For a moment she fantasized about stripping him down and making love right there in the entryway, but reality, and the nine-year-old boy sleeping down the hall, brought her to her senses. Pulling away reluctantly, she dragged him into the kitchen, where she had poured herself a well-earned glass of wine.

"Want one?" She lifted her glass in question.

"What I want," he thundered, "is to know what kind of game it is you're playing!"

She stepped back, sloshing wine onto the floor. "What? What do you mean? I'm not playing any game."

"No? What do you call it, then, when you disappear for days with no warning, refuse to answer my calls, basically ignore the fact that we ever met, and then, when you finally get back, rather than explain what the hell is going on, you jump me at the front door?"

She cringed, hearing the hurt behind his anger. Setting down her glass, she took a deep breath. She had more explaining to do than she'd realized.

"Maybe we should sit down."

"No, I'll stand, thanks."

All right. Fine. "First, I'm sorry I didn't tell you where I was going. Honestly, I didn't think you'd even miss me."

"Seriously?" He shoved a hand through his hair, making lines in the damp locks. "I've been out of my mind! I held out for a day, but then when I went by your office and you weren't there—"

"You went by my office?" She hadn't expected that.

"Yeah, I did. I brought you flowers."

Guilt sunk like a stone in her belly. She really had messed up. Somehow, she'd pictured him going on with his life, with work and the girls, and just not really thinking about her at all. Obviously she'd been wrong.

"I don't know if I should say 'thank you' or 'I'm sorry.'"

He sunk down into the nearest kitchen chair and shook his head. "I don't know, either."

He sounded tired and worn down. And she'd been the one to do this to him. "Well, let's start with I'm sorry. I really didn't think you'd miss me. And I did say I was going to be busy."

"There's a big difference between busy and vanished, Dani."

"You're right." She saw now that she'd under-estimated him, and his feelings for her. Which on one hand made her feel awful, but on the other, meant he really did care about her. Letting that flicker of hope burn, she tried again. "I should have told you I was leaving. And I would have, but I was afraid you'd want to go with me, and I needed to do this myself."

"Do what yourself? You still haven't told me where you were, or why you left."

Darn it, she was getting to that. Better to just spit it out and then explain afterward. "I went to Jacksonville and filed formal charges against the man that attacked me."

His jaw dropped. "You did? How did it go? Are you okay?"

She laughed, glad that some of the tension had dissolved with her news. "Yes, I did. And it went as well as can be expected, I guess. It will be a while before I know if they are going to arrest him, but he'll at least be brought in for questioning. And as for me, I'm fantastic. At least, I was before I realized how much I put you through." That she felt terribly about. She should have given him more credit. Really, she should have given their relationship more credit.

"Yeah, well, I survived. Barely," he added with a grin. "I thought you'd left town because you wanted to break up, or maybe you were moving away permanently. Hell, I didn't know what to think."

Now it was her turn to be shocked. "Break up? Why on earth would you think that?"

"Well, you left town without telling me, and then you wouldn't return my calls or my texts. What was I supposed to think?"

"That I had something to take care of, would tell you about it when I got back." When he started to protest she held up a hand, silencing him. "I get now that

I was wrong. I do. But Tyler, I promise you, me leaving had nothing to do with you. I love you."

Silently, he stood. Did he not believe her? Was he going to walk out? But then, before she could ask him to say something, anything, he grabbed her and pulled her into his arms, his mouth coming down hard on hers. The kiss was possessive, primitive—and it curled her toes and heated her body. When he backed away she had to grip the edge of the counter to keep upright. "Wow. Does that mean you forgive me?"

He shook his head, a boyish grin creeping across his face. "Oh, no, not yet. You put me through hell, woman. And I still don't know why you didn't return my calls."

She felt her face flush. "It sounds stupid now, but I just wanted to tell you in person."

He laughed. "Okay, that I didn't think of." Growing more serious, he motioned her over to sit beside him. "So, now that we're both here, tell me all about it."

She explained how she had tracked down other women that had worked there, and found out that she wasn't the only one he'd abused.

"Wait, you've been working on this for that long? Why didn't you say anything?"

"I didn't know yet if I was actually going to do anything with the information. I didn't want you to think badly of me if I ended up just dropping the whole thing."

"Never." He took her hand and squeezed it. "This was always your call to make. No one can second-guess what's right for you."

"Thanks." That meant a lot. She'd been judging herself for so long, she didn't need anyone else doing it, too.

"So, how bad was it? Had any of them been…"

"Raped? No. But he tried with another one. He would have, if the janitor hadn't come in on a different day than was scheduled. She quit just about a month before I was hired."

"Wow." He sat back in his chair, no doubt realizing how much worse it could have been—both for the other woman and for her. "I know I just said that it was your decision, as far as pressing charges, and I meant that. But now that you have, I'm glad you did. That sicko needs to be put where he can't hurt anyone else."

She nodded. "I know. But that's not the only reason I did it. I also wanted to prove to myself it was over. When we told Kevin that you have to face your problems if you want to get past them, I realize I had to do that myself. And I did."

"And do you feel you are past it now?"

"In a way, I do. I'll still have to deal with my PTSD—that won't go away overnight. But it's getting better, and I think this will be a big help. I feel safer, in general, now that people know. I even told my family."

"Good. So I guess the next question is, where do you go from here?"

She shrugged. "I don't know, exactly. But I know whatever I do, wherever I go, it's going to be with you. Because, Tyler Jackson, I love you."

"Well that's good. Because I love you too, Dani. But you have to promise no more running off without telling me—I can't take that again."

"I promise." From now on she was going to focus on the future. And as Tyler took her into his arms she knew he was definitely a part of any future she could imagine.

Chapter Fifteen

Tyler felt like he was living in a very strange fairy tale. Not because of his relationship with Dani, although that was hopefully about to steer into happily-ever-after territory. But because he was currently surrounded by two princesses and a knight in shining armor.

It was a slow day at the shop, and Kevin had come by to hang out while Dani was at her therapy appointment. She'd wanted to fit in some extra visits after everything that happened in Jacksonville and he'd encouraged her to do so, which meant for the past month and a half he'd often picked up Kevin from school when he got the girls. The kids had shared a snack and were now playing dress up. Kevin had been reluctant to play such a "girly" game, as he put it, until Tyler found him the knight costume. Now he was brandishing a sword and defending the princesses from imaginary dragons, as into the pretend play as the younger kids.

Their antics helped to keep Tyler's mind occupied, but even as he alternated between playing the prince and the evil ogre, he was watching the door, waiting for Dani. But that was how it was now. No matter what he was doing, or where he was, at least some part of him was thinking about her. She was the new constant that gave his life direction and meaning. He wasn't just a father; he was a man in love with a woman. And somehow, he was lucky enough to be loved back.

How that had happened, he still wasn't sure. Maybe the kids were on to something. Maybe there was such a thing as magic. Because how else could you explain it? At their very first meeting she'd pegged him as the enemy, a man with a heart of stone. As evil as the villains in the fairy-tale books he sold. And his snap judgment of her hadn't been much better. He'd though her attractive but naive, someone who liked to say they were helping while actually just getting in the way.

And he couldn't have been more wrong. Well, except for the attractive part. She was drop-dead gorgeous and that hadn't changed. But she was anything but naive. She had a brilliant mind, which, combined with her never-give-up attitude, made her a force to be reckoned with. No doubt in the days ahead there would be times when they would butt heads—they were both too opinionated to not do so—but he couldn't think of anyone else he'd rather disagree with.

The bell at the front door announced a new arrival, and even before he turned he knew it was her. He could somehow feel her presence whenever she was near. And in the time since her trip to Jacksonville, he'd made sure she was near as often as possible. They'd started eating dinner together with all the kids several nights a week, as well as making trips to the playground; even grocery shopping had become something they found they enjoyed more when done together. And while Tyler helped Kevin with his batting practice, the girls were soaking up some female bonding time with Dani. They'd even managed to finally squeeze in a few real dates without the kids, thanks to the number of people who had come forward offering to babysit. Of course, finding real privacy was another issue all together. After they'd been caught by Amy sneaking hand in hand into the bedroom one night they'd been resigned to making out on the couch like teenagers. Something his libido was not happy about, but a problem he was hoping to rectify sooner rather than later.

"How was your appointment?" He didn't like to pry, but he did want to stay informed as to her progress. And so far, she'd been grateful for his interest. They'd even arranged one couples' session, which had gone really well. He had more tips now, on how to help her if she had a panic attack or bad spell and a new understanding of how far she'd come.

"Good." She smiled and set her purse behind the counter. "We're going to cut back to monthly visits, see how that goes. She called me one of her success stories."

"That's great." Pride swelled inside him, not only at her progress, but also her candor in discussing it. She was no longer embarrassed, and had even talked about having her therapist address the women in the workplace group she was forming.

"Thanks. But seeing you is even better." She gave him a quick kiss and then stood next to him, shoulders touching, as they watched the kids play. "They're pretty good therapy, too. What are they doing?"

"Playing out a fairy tale. And I think it's only fair you join in." He turned to the kids. "What do you say— can Dani be part of the game?"

Dani let herself be dragged into the game, accepting a glittery tiara from Adelaide and an "almost real" magic wand from Amy. Kevin bowed before her, and she laughed as his helmet fell shut over his eyes. What really tickled her, though, was seeing Tyler get into the act. He had found a cape of some sort, and to the girl's delight announced himself to be Prince Charming, come to woo Dani, the sleeping princess.

"First, you have to get by me!" declared Kevin, darting in front of him with his sword drawn.

Taking the bait, Tyler grabbed a child's broom from the display beside him, sparring his way closer to Dani. When they were nearly at her feet, Tyler leaned down to whisper something in Kevin's ear. Eyes aglow, Kevin nodded and lowered his sword, bowing to the "prince."

"Hey, you're supposed to be asleep, remember?" Amy complained, a stickler for propriety. "He can't wake you from the spell if you're already awake."

Sufficiently chastised, Dani closed her eyes as Tyler pretended to climb up a tower to get to her.

"At last, I've found my princess." She could hear his voice, close now, and shivered a bit at the emotion in it. He sounded much more serious than she'd expect from a man playing pretend.

"Now you have to kiss her, Daddy," Adelaide explained. "That's how the prince wakes her up."

She'd forgotten that part of the story. They hadn't made of habit of kissing in front of the kids, although at this point their relationship was far from secret. Still, it fit with the story, so she'd just enjoy it and not worry. Holding her breath, she waited, and was rewarded with a tender press of lips, a gentle kiss that spoke of love and friendship and happily ever after all rolled up in one. Sighing, she nearly forgot to open her eyes, until Kevin spoke up. "Um, you're supposed to be awake now."

Obediently, she did as told, and then blinked in surprise. At her feet, down on one knee, was Tyler. Was that part of the story? It must be. Playing along, she smiled down at him as majestically as possible. "Thank you for saving me, handsome prince. I'm so grateful."

"Truthfully, you're the one who saved me. Before I met you, I was only living a shadow of a life. And now that I have you, I never want to let you go." He took a small box out of his pocket, and opened it. The incoming sunlight from the window shattered into dozens of rainbows as it hit the jeweled ring inside.

Offering her hand, she let him place the ring on her finger, and then froze. She wasn't a diamond expert, but even she could tell, this was no children's plaything. But if the ring was real, did that mean the proposal was? "Um, Tyler?" She looked back to him, and saw only sincerity in his eyes.

"Yes, it's real," he said, answering her unspoken question. "The ring, and the proposal. I've spent too many years buried within myself, and then I met you and everything changed. You make me a better man, and a better father. And I want to be those things with you. Forever. You've brought sunshine and laughter and hope into my life."

"And kittens!" Adelaide added.

"And kittens," he acknowledged with a grin. "And we want all of those things, all of us. But most of all, we want you. So Dani Post, will you do me the honor of marrying me, so you and I and the kids can all live happily ever after, together?"

Tears clouded her vision as she nodded, too full of emotion to speak. Finally, swallowing back the happy tears that threatened to choke her, she answered him. "Yes. Absolutely yes."

The kids cheered, but she barely heard them. Tyler was all she could focus on, as he rose, her hand in his, and brought her in for another kiss. "I don't think this is part of the story, Tyler," she whispered against his lips.

"We're making our own fairy tale now. And not all of it is going to be suitable for children."

He kissed her for real then, spurring hoots and hollers of delight from not only the children, but also a family of customers who had walked in without them noticing.

Tyler, hearing them, pulled away reluctantly, and she couldn't help but laugh at the look of frustration on his face. "Don't worry, Prince Charming. This story is definitely going to be continued."

Chapter Sixteen

Three months later...

As quickly as their love had bloomed, it turned out that weddings couldn't be rushed. Not if they wanted to have all their family and friends there, and have time for at least a brief honeymoon. Between their jobs, the kids' schedules and the ordinary details that went with planning such an event, it was summer by the time Dani put on her dress and prepared to walk down the aisle. Surrounding her in the makeshift bride's room, otherwise known as Jillian's bedroom at the Sandpiper Inn, were some of the most important people in her life. Mollie, her matron of honor was there of course, and her friends, Jillian, Sam, Cassie, and Cassie's sister-in-law, Jessica had insisted on crowding in too for moral support.

The only missing members were the twins, who

were so excited about being flower girls that they'd had to be taken outside to run off some energy. Emma, Cassie's daughter, had helped them practice for the role, and was acting as a junior bridesmaid. Kevin was off with the men, having been chosen by Tyler to be his best man. The ceremony itself was going to be down on the beach, after they'd realized that the gazebo they'd originally planned to use was too small to hold the bride and groom and the kids.

And the kids would be up there, front and center with them. Both Tyler and Dani had agreed that this wasn't just the joining of a couple, but the joining of two families. It only made sense then, to fully include all members equally.

"Hey, honey, it's time." Her father poked his head around the bedroom door. "The music is starting, and everyone is in place."

Butterflies did an interpretive dance in her stomach, in time with the rushed rhythm of her pulse. She had no regrets regarding Tyler; she knew she loved him more than she'd ever known anything. But this, this was a huge step, not just for her, but for their families. Were they doing the right thing by them? Were they really ready for all this?

In answer, the two most precious little girls in the world appeared, rushing through the door to grab her hands. "Come on, Dani! It's starting!" Adelaide pulled her, trying to force her to keep up.

"Yeah, Dani. We need to hurry so you can be our mom. Dad said we could call you that afterward, if it was okay with you." Amy blinked bright blue eyes up at her, and just like that, any last-minute fears were washed away. "Is it okay?"

"Absolutely. I'd love that."

"Dani Post, don't you dare cry," Cassie ordered, dabbing at her own eyes. "You'll spoil your makeup."

"I won't." She was too happy to cry even happy tears. Bless those kids for reminding her again that love was greater than fear. "Come on, girls, we've got a wedding to go to."

They took the stairs down to the beach hand in hand, only letting go when it was time for the girls to take their baskets of petals. Her father stepped beside her then, her past catching up to her future. "Dani, before we go, I just want you to know I'm not just happy for you, I'm proud of you. I know Tyler will take good care of you, but more importantly, I know you can take care of yourself. You've turned into an amazing woman, and I love you."

Now the tears did come, but she didn't care. Today wasn't about makeup and dresses—it was about people. And she was lucky enough to be surrounded by ones she loved, and that loved her. "Thank you, Daddy. I love you, too."

The music changed, and now it was their turn. With her arm in his, she and her father started down the white runner that had been placed on the sand. White chairs on either side held a good portion of the island's population, and down by the water, waiting for her, was Tyler, looking even more like a fairy-tale hero. His white dress shirt was open at the neck, creating a contrast with the tanned skin underneath. When he saw her in her dress, the one she'd been hiding from him for months, his eyes widened.

She'd gone for the full princess effect, despite the casual setting. It had a tight bodice that scooped low between her breasts, and a full skirt that swirled and swished when she walked. Her hair was too short to be worn in a fancy updo, so instead she wore a small tiara in honor of the one she'd worn when he proposed, albeit less plastic and more grown-up looking. In total, she felt like royalty, and the look in Tyler's eyes said he agreed with the sentiment.

She kissed her father goodbye, and then took her place at Tyler's side. The officiant, a local judge and longtime family friend, conducted the ceremony, using the words they had chosen. Then it was time for the vows. She and Tyler stuck with the traditional version, pledging to love, honor and cherish each other as long as they both lived. Then the kids stepped forward, and new vows that they had written as a family were recited. She and Tyler promised to love, guide, protect and care for each of the children, and in return the kids vowed to love and care for their new parent and siblings. Each of them received a medallion on a chain, depicting the family crest she and Tyler had designed. They both hoped to formally adopt Kevin, and Kevin wanted that too, but it was a long process that could take up to a year. In the meantime, the medallions would be a symbol of their solidarity.

And then, vows over and no objections raised, she kissed her groom.

No inhibitions, no embarrassment; she kissed him like she meant it. They were married, and darn it, she intended to make the most of it. When they came up for air the crowd was on their feet clapping and the girls were giggling in embarrassment. Kevin, the poor boy, just rolled his eyes.

Walking down the aisle, they went as a family, five

across, drawing even more cheers and applause. Mollie, who'd traded her bouquet for a camera the instant the ceremony ended, captured them, all together, and gave a thumbs-up. They'd done it. They were a family, and nothing could tear them apart now.

Except of course, for the honeymoon. That evening, after the party was over and it was just her and Tyler on the boat they'd rented, she was perfectly happy to have this little portion of their marriage be child-free. Her mom and Tyler's mother were taking turns watching the kids for the next three days, after which the kids would join them for a family vacation on the water.

But for now, they had the cozy cabin all to themselves. And the heat in Tyler's eyes said he intended to make the most of it. She didn't blame him...they'd waited a long time to consummate this relationship. Sipping the champagne he'd poured, bubbles tickling her nose, she turned her back to him. "Think you can help get me out of this? There are a whole lot of buttons."

"I'll get it off if I have to chew through it," he growled, his breath hot on her neck as he undid one small button after another. He kissed his way down her back, anointing each new bit of flesh as he uncovered it. By the time he finished she was holding her breath in anticipation, afraid to move and spoil the moment.

He parted the dress, exposing more of her skin, letting it fall from her shoulders to puddle in a pool of satin and tulle at her feet. "Beautiful. But I want to see all of you."

Obliging, she turned to him, removing the lacy scraps of fabric the bridal boutique had convinced her to buy. She shouldn't have bothered; he was definitely more interested in her than the lingerie. His eyes dark and stormy, he led her to the bed and proceeded to show her exactly how much more interested he was. The first time they came together it was explosive, each pushing the other to go faster and harder, needing that feeling of completeness that only complete union could bring. Then, moving gently along with the rocking of the boat, they started all over again, taking the time to explore every inch of each other's bodies.

Later, lying in the dark, the starlight shining through the open porthole, Dani whispered a prayer of gratitude to the vast sky above. She'd found her prince, and she'd found her strength, and as far as she was concerned, that was what happily ever after was all about.

* * * * *

If you loved this novel, don't miss
A WEDDING WORTH WAITING FOR,
the first title in Katie Meyer's
PROPOSALS IN PARADISE *miniseries.*

And be sure to pick up the other stories in the
author's PARADISE ANIMAL CLINIC *miniseries:*

DO YOU TAKE THIS DADDY?
A VALENTINE FOR THE VETERINARIAN
THE PUPPY PROPOSAL

Available now from Harlequin Special Edition!

Dear Reader,

This month—April 2017—marks the 35th anniversary for Harlequin Special Edition! Perhaps it's as hard for you, the reader, to believe this as it is for us, the team that has been presenting this warm, wonderful and relatable series of books for all these years. And while some of us are newer than others, the one thing that has always been consistent is that the Harlequin Special Edition lineup has always reached out and grabbed you, made you want to read more, made you look forward to what comes next.

April 2017 is a great illustration of this. We have *New York Times* bestselling author Brenda Novak in Harlequin Special Edition for the first time with *Finding Our Forever*, alongside our almost-brand-new author Katie Meyer with another in her Proposals in Paradise series, *The Groom's Little Girls*. We have *USA TODAY* bestselling and beloved authors Marie Ferrarella (*Meant to be Married*) and Judy Duarte in our next Fortunes of Texas: The Secret Fortunes story (*From Fortune to Family Man*). And if it's glamour, glitz and sparkle you want with your romance, look no further than *The Princess Problem* (next in the Drake Diamonds trilogy) by Teri Wilson.

We have moved through the last thirty-five years giving you, the reader, stories that warmed your heart and curled your toes, and we are just getting started! So happy anniversary...and here's to the next thirty-five!

Happy Reading,

Gail Chasan
Senior Editor, Harlequin Special Edition

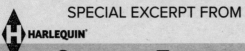
"Mirabelle's?" It was a new restaurant in town, a small, cozy place with white tablecloths and crystal chandeliers and a chef from New York. Everyone said the food was really good and the service impeccable.

"I heard it was good," he said. "Would you rather go somewhere else?"

"I just didn't know we were doing that."

"Doing what?"

"Going through with the date."

He set down his fork. "We're doing it." His voice was deep and rough, and his velvet-brown gaze caught hers and held it.

It just wasn't fair that the guy was so damn hot. *Not happening*, she reminded herself. *Don't get ideas.* "What about Marybeth?"

"It's only a few hours. Get a sitter. Maybe one of your sisters or maybe your mom?"

"Ma? Please."

"She did raise five children, didn't she?"

"She's probably off on her next cruise already."

"A babysitter, Jody. I'm sure you can find one."

"But Marybeth is barely four weeks old."

"Jody. We're going. Stop making excuses."

She sagged back in her chair. "Why are you so determined about this?"

"Because I want to take you out."

"But…you don't go out, remember? There's no point because it can't go anywhere. Not to mention, I live in Broomtail County, and what if it got messy with me?"

"Too late." He was almost smiling. She could see that increasingly familiar twitch at the corner of his mouth. "It's already messy with you."

"I am not joking, Seth."

"Neither am I. I want to be with you, Jody. And not just as a friend."

"B-but I…" God. She was sputtering. And why did she suddenly feel light as a breath of air, as if she was floating on moonbeams? "You want to be with me? But you don't do that. You've made that very clear."

"You're right. I didn't do that. Until now. But things have changed."

"Because of Marybeth, you mean?"

"Yeah, because of Marybeth. And because of you, too. Because of the way you are. Strong and honest and smart and so pretty. Because we've got something going on, you and me. Something good. I'm through pretending that we're friends and nothing more. Are you telling me I'm the only one who feels that way?"

"I just…" Her pulse raced and her cheeks felt too hot. She'd promised herself that nothing like this would happen, that she wouldn't get her hopes up.

She needed to be careful. She could end up with her heart in pieces all over again.

Don't miss
THE LAWMAN'S CONVENIENT BRIDE
by Christine Rimmer, available May 2017 wherever
Harlequin® Special Edition books and ebooks are sold.

www.Harlequin.com

$7.99 U.S./$9.99 CAN.

$1.00 OFF

New York Times
bestselling author
brenda novak

welcomes you to Silver
Springs, a picturesque small
town in Southern California
where even the hardest hearts
can learn to love again...

MIRA®

Available May 30, 2017.

$1.00 OFF

the purchase price of **NO ONE BUT YOU**
by Brenda Novak.

Offer valid from May 30, 2017, to June 30, 2017.
Redeemable at participating retail outlets, in-store only. Not redeemable at
Barnes & Noble. Limit one coupon per purchase. Valid in the U.S.A. and Canada only.

52614662

5 65373 00076 2 (8100)0 12267

® and ™ are trademarks owned and used by the trademark owner and/or its licensee.

© 2017 Harlequin Enterprises Limited

MCOUPBN0617

Get 2 Free Books,

Plus 2 Free Gifts—

just for trying the Reader Service!

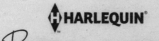